BONFIRES
OF
THE
GODS

a novel

Andrew Eseimokumo Oki

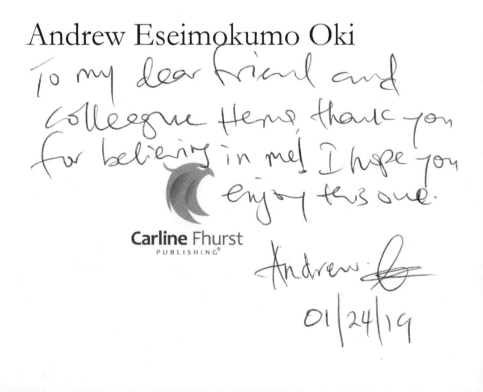

To my dear friend and colleague Hems, thank you for believing in me! I hope you enjoy this one.

Andrew

01/24/19

Carline Fhurst
PUBLISHING®

First edition published by Serene Woods, India, 2011
Second edition published by Griots Lounge, Nigeria, 2012

Published in the United States by Carline Fhurst Publishing LLC, New Jersey.

info@carlinefhurstpublishing.com

The Phoenix colophon is a trademark of Carline Fhurst Publishing LLC.

Library of Congress Cataloging-in-Publication Data is available upon request.

ISBN – 978-1-791-68723-6

Printed in the United States of America

Book cover design by Fred Martins
Author photograph by Thierry Tamfu

For Etipou and Denyefa; the ones we've lost.

For my beloved city, Warri.

For my beloved Abonomor.

"Power and violence are opposites; where one rules absolutely, the other is absent. Violence appears where power is in jeopardy, but if left to its own cause, it ends in power's disappearance."

HANNAH ARENDT

Praise for *Bonfires of the gods.*

Oki weaves an intricate yet impressive narrative with a deftness that befits practiced hands. In "Bonfires of the gods", an important contribution to the Niger Delta discourse, our frailty as a nation comes to fore, as ethnicity erodes community. – Uche Peter Umez, author of Tears in Her Eyes

"Bonfires of the gods" is very well written and quite deeply researched; the author shows off his creative chops and interweaves it with hands-on knowledge of the area he is writing about. – Myne Whitman, Managing Editor, Naijastories.com

"Bonfires of the gods" is hot. It is one thing to be a storyteller and another thing to be a story-shower. Andrew Eseimokumo Oki possesses both powers, but as you listen to his voice, you will find all the necessary requisites integral to a good story. What makes this an extraordinary story is the ordinary style by this writer. I loved it. – Onyeka Nwelue, Author *"The Abyssinian Boy"*.

Andrew Eseimokumo Oki has shown his strength as a griot, delving into a theme so daring in such a captivating manner. Every page brings new people and gets you reading. Here is a brilliant debut. – Binyerem Ukonu, Author *"The Water was Hot"*.

"Bonfires of the gods", true to its nature, is uniquely African, a beautifully told story and very quintessentially historical and true to the African experience… – Urban Royale Magazine

"Bonfires of the gods" is certainly a work that should be given
its due significance for taking on the much-needed task of urging
Nigerians to remember those events in their past that though
unhappy should not be forgotten. – Brittle Paper, UK

Being a witness to the unnecessary crimes associated with the ethnic
wars between the Ijaws and Itsekiris in 1997, I could relate with
the deep, yet unbiased emotions depicted in this high work of art
"Bonfires of the gods" - Dele Elempe, Author *"Season of*
Imperfection".

Oki's "Bonfires of the gods" is not only thrilling and informative, it
is one of the best war stories ever told in recent times as it
beautifully weaves love, friendship, loyalty and intense romance into
a heartrending war story. With this debut, Andrew Eseimokumo
Oki boldly pens his name in the list of burgeoning contemporary
African writers. – Echezonachukwu Nduka for Bella Naija

…Centered on subjects as gruesome as inter-ethnic rivalry and war,
it is amazing how Oki can weave love, friendship, marriage and
loyalty into the story…. - Amara Chimeka, Literary Critic.

Prologue.

Duwamabou.

IT RAINED THE DAY I DIED. Every drop that fell on the zinc roofing sheets sounded like pebbles landing on my head. I felt a quiver, like the building was shaking. Or, was it my body shuddering?

Rain.

I often wondered what the phenomenon behind it was. God was crying up in heaven. Who knew? I wondered why He would choose a day like that to cry. I couldn't say. Sometimes, I don't even remember He's up there.

The rain poured on with incredible ferociousness. Maybe a leak in heaven's water banks, and Earth was suffering the consequences. Whatever it was, I didn't know. I decided to leave it to the rainmakers to figure out.

The downpour never stopped that day.

I always knew Warri was a no-go area when it rained. I turned to look at the window, thinking I would see a bit of the city outside. Instead, I saw streaks of tear-like water flowing down the window glass. It caught my attention. *Even the windows were crying for me!* I smiled. My eyes were closing, and still I could count the streaks on the glass. It was a funny feeling. I thought I could see myself laughing.

One, two, three, four... I tried to keep count, but each time, new streaks replaced the old ones. I knew it was foolish to account for such things, but somehow it gave me hope. It kept my mind busy. It was as if it could take the pain away, and I held on to it with more faith than I had in the doses of morphine pumping through my dying body.

The storm continued. Loud cracking thunderclaps chased after flashes of lightning like children playing in the sand banks of the River Niger in Patani.

I remembered when my childhood friends and I used to say that thunderclaps were the result of applauses in heaven. We believed that wars happened because the gods of the Earth felt cold and stopped watching over us to gather large trees to make bonfires to keep themselves warm. How young we were! We knew these theories were baseless and silly, but we believed them, anyway.

My eyelids drooped in a slow-motion blink. I looked around, and for the first time it occurred to me that I was in a hospital. I could not move my body, but it trembled in pain. How I got there was a mystery to me. My memory was still in fragmented pieces. I remembered waking in my own bed that morning, breathing in the fresh air and looking forward to a wonderful day. I remembered the warm shower I took, a stark contrast to the cold rain outside. I'd hated the shirt I'd picked out to wear for work, but I wore it anyway. I did not have many shirts. I remembered having jollof rice with moi-moi. It was my favorite and my mother knew that. I also remembered the screams and the running. There was fire, consuming everything in its path, and the sounds of gunshots. Then, darkness.

From my periphery, I could see two nurses talking. I had no idea what they said to each other. I guessed it was about me, because one of them soon came over to my bedside.

She had a pretty oval-shaped face, smooth, hot-chocolate colored skin and cherry red lips. Her beautiful black hair sat atop her head in well-cultivated corn-rows. She had no make-up on, but her face shone like dark colored honey. I noticed the tiny beautiful gold pins she had for earrings. Her slim neck was bare and smooth.

I absorbed all these thoughts in what seemed like forever, as she looked down upon my face. If only I wasn't so dead on that bed, what all I could do…

I could give her pleasure that would send her to high heavens and kiss her lips to nothingness, replacing them with that of the goddess Athena's and she would keep wanting more every minute of every passing day.

What I could do …

She bent over me to examine my body, her sumptuous breasts dangling right in front of my face, as she checked my vitals. Even though I was dying, I realized there was a part of me that wasn't so dead and weak. That part cheered and nudged in agreement between my thighs. I could feel its solidification. I wished I could lay claim to the bounty set before me.

Her breasts hung over me, in lovely contrast to the certain death that loomed over my head. I began to think of what my passing would feel like and where I was going to end up. Was I going to heaven or hell? Or, would I spend some quality time in *Duwamabou* with my grandmother beside me, helping me think about what my life could have been? I shivered at the thought. I could not feel my legs anymore, and I very much wanted to give pleasure to the beautiful young nurse. Yet, nothing mattered to me as much as the fear of going to *Duwamabou*.

Duwamabou! I was just a child when I first heard that word. It was the funniest Ijaw word I'd ever heard. Of course, that was before I knew what it meant. I liked the musical pronunciation of the word. It sounded like "drummer boy" to me. My siblings and I didn't speak much of our native Ijaw language. Pidgin English was our primary language. So, like other children, the quickest and easiest Ijaw words we picked up were those of acute vulgarity. *Duwamabou* was one of them.

Duwamabou, or the "halfway house," was neither heaven nor hell, according to what we grew up believing. It was a place where the spirits of the dead went to handle their "unfinished" business before passing on to their eternal afterlife. As for me, I never understood the whole concept of *Duwamabou*. However, as I lay there dying, I thought of *Duwamabou* for what seemed like hours.

Was my dead grandmother still there? She'd been dead for ten years. She must've settled her unfinished business and moved from the 'halfway house.' Could she still be there? Would I see her when, or if, I got there? What would I tell her? '*What brings you knocking on Duwamabou's door?*' I imagined her asking me in her stern voice, with all the love in the world reflecting in her eyes. I realized I did not want to die. Not for the normal reasons why people don't want to die. Of all things, I was afraid of not having a reasonable explanation for my granny if she asked me what I was doing in *Duwamabou.*

My nurse began speaking to a woman wearing a white coat. I had not seen the white-coated woman there before. I could not hear what my beautiful nurse was saying, but I saw the white-coated woman rush towards my bed. I could see blurry images before my eyes. I turned again to look at the window. It was still raining, I guessed, but I could not hear the rain drops anymore. I looked for the streaks of rainwater, but it was difficult to adjust my focus. I began to panic. Thoughts of *Duwamabou* still raced through my head.

God, what was happening?

The white-coated woman shoved the nurse away and placed her palms on my chest. She began to push hard. I could not feel anything. I could not move, but I knew I was still alive. I didn't want to close my eyes, for fear that they would never open again. I was looking up, but instead of the ceiling, I saw clouds in a beautiful blue sky. I tried to smile. I could not hear the commotion around me, but I could see the doctors fight to save my life.

Now I could only hear the chirps of birds. I could see a fleet of birds flying in the clouds above my bed.

Just as I was beginning to smile at the beauty around me, the blue sky began to darken and fade. It happened so fast I could not comprehend it. I looked on still as the sky turned black. I panicked.

Oh God!

I had lost my streaks of rainwater on the window.

Gone was my beautiful nurse with the pair of sumptuous breasts.

My magical white-blue sky had vanished.

I lost all hope.

Then I knew that I was dead, and on my way to *Duwamabou*.

God! What would I tell grandmother?

Warri, Nigeria
March 1997.

One.

Tonye and Laju

GRANDMOTHER WAS A LITTLE CRAZY, everyone knew that.

Everyone feared to approach her doorstep, let alone knock. People wondered if anyone ever visited her. Of course, people did. People always visited grandmother. She was the heart and soul of the Itsekiri community in Warri. She was *everyone's* mother, if a little intimidating. Grandmother commanded a great deal of respect, and she did so with such grace and poise that some wondered what supernatural entity bestowed it upon her.

When people visited, she always insisted they remove their footwear before stepping into her house. She called her living room her "Persian living room," because of the wall-to-wall expensive, hand-made Persian rugs she had had shipped from Cairo, Egypt during one of her trips abroad.

Even when the Delta State Military Administrator had visited and hadn't removed his shoes, Grandmother had performed her usual drama before him. Before his arrival, she had asked one of her maids to show him in. She reminded the maid to make sure to ask him to remove his shoes. The maid was so embarrassed by the errand and afraid of the man's personage that she had just let him in, mumbling a meek, "Welcome, sir." When grandmother noticed he had his shoes on, she questioned the maid about it, in his presence. The governor apologized on the maid's behalf and offered to remove his shoes. Grandmother turned to him and smiled.

"Don't mind my maid. Sometimes, she forgets these things," She said.

That was who grandmother was. To us, she was just grandmother. To the rest of the community, she was Chief Oritsegbene Dawson.

People used her name with great respect, including her own children. She was a strong woman who ran her household with an iron fist, but no one could measure the love she had for her children and grandchildren. And she would go to any length to prove it.

*

"Are you sure your grandma will like me? I've heard so many things about her, and I'm a little scared," Tonye said, smiling.

"You worry too much, Tonye. She'll love you. My grandma may be old fashioned but a brute and a bigot - she is not," Laju said. She rubbed her fiancé's head.

"I sure hope so. Where do I turn?" He asked, teasing, as they approached a road sign that read "Oritsegbene Dawson Drive."

11

"Yeah, right. Very funny."

"Wow! Don't tell me everyone living on this street is Itsekiri," Tonye said. He looked from side to side as he drove down the beautiful boulevard.

"Well, not everyone. We have some Urhobo's, Yoruba's, and of course, the Tolani's."

"Yeah, the couple you told me about. The man is Itsekiri and his wife is Ijaw. It is an Itsekiri family now, so the combo doesn't exclude them."

"I hear you *Lawyer Nwanjoku*!" She said, laughing.

"Heavens, please don't call me that. Any other lawyer *yabing* will do, but please baby, not the *Nwanjoku* one," Tonye said.

"Oh! I see someone doesn't like his name ehn."

"Baby *abeg* stop am."

"We're here."

"Sorry?"

"I said we're here. Look, that's Grandma's house," she said, pointing to a mansion just across the street.

"Wow! *That* is your grandmother's house?" Tonye asked, his mouth agape.

"Yep, it is. Close your mouth honey," Laju said.

Tonye closed his mouth, embarrassed.

"And remember…" Laju said.

"I know, I know. 'Remove your shoes before entering my Persian living room,' blah blah blah. She for *kuku* import the whole living room from China na," he said. They both laughed as he turned off the ignition.

"Honey, behave," Laju said, composing herself.

"I will. Gosh, your grandmother's house is beautiful. And here I was thinking that my grandparents had the most beautiful house on Earth," he said.

"In your mind. Which house? You mean the spread of huts they built in the late 17th Century?" Laju said. Tonye was cracking her up.

Tonye grew serious, silence replacing his humor.

After a few quiet moments, the couple exited the car and stared up at the house.

Tonye regarded the house with awe. Chief Oritsegbene Dawson's mansion was of modern architecture. Tonye could see the entire building from across the road where they parked, because the block fence wasn't very high. Above, the blocks were elegant see-through iron bars.

Anyone approaching the mansion might expect to see a queen. Tonye sure felt that way. The design was French, but it resembled something from the Gregorian era. Tonye recognized the style from spending too much time reading *Architectural Digest*. The French windows held the rising sun captive. The mirrored glasses threw sunlight over the beautiful green front lawn. The lush carpet of grass left an imprint of its color on the guest's retinas. Around the lawn and house were beautiful flowers. A red brick-interlocked pathway led straight to the huge entrance door. Grand red roses guarded the grandiose entrance. A golden knocker in the shape of a lion's head adorned the door. Tonye swallowed. It was too much for him to take in all at once.

Laju Dawson used the lion-head knocker. Three heavy thuds brought Tonye back to earth. He had been so enthralled by the mansion, he hadn't realized that they already stood at the door.

They heard someone struggling to open the door. Tonye felt like he was in a real-life version of *Alice in the Wonderland*. All at once, the door seemed much bigger. He was afraid of what to expect from the popular old lady everyone regarded with such fearful respect.

"Eeeeeeeeeeeeeee! Auntie Laju! Auntie Laju! Welcome," a lady said as she realized who it was. She appeared to be one of grandmother's maids. Tonye wondered if she was the one who had let in the Colonel without asking him to remove his shoes. Perhaps that one may have been relieved of her duties and sent on her way.

"How are you Mabel? Mama dey house so? Is mama at home?" Laju asked as they removed their shoes and stepped into the house.

"Ehn. She no dey. She comot since but she talk sey make una wait for am when una come. Na meeting she go." the maid said, knocking the sand off their shoes and placing them inside the hallway.

"Of course, we will wait. Na she make us come Warri o. Ehn Mabel, come and meet my husband-to-be," Laju said.

"Ewoooooo. Oga abeg no vex." Mabel said, kneeling in front of Tonye. Embarrassed, he addressed the maid.

"Please get up Mabel. I'm Tonye Kemefa. It's nice to meet you."

Tonye saw the smile fade from the maid's face at the mention of his name. She picked herself up, trying to hide it. He wasn't surprised.

"You're welcome sir. Please come inside o," Mabel said. "What would you like to drink?" The maid led them through the hallway to the famed 'Persian living room.'

Tonye couldn't help but notice that the décor was rather traditional and not over the top as he had imagined. A tiny strip of sunlight streamed in through a window into the hallway. On a wooden cabinet stood sat a white crystal vase bearing a mixture of fresh tulips and hibiscus flowers in a vast array of colors.

On the wall to the right were six portraits of all of grandmother's six children with their spouses.

"These are my uncles and aunties with their spouses in the order of birth." Laju said. She had to offer an explanation when she saw a puzzled look on Tonye's face. Lajus's parents were number five.

The banister of the staircase had a striking ironwork, emphasizing the sweeping curves that drew Tonye's eyes up at a five-arm Amrose chandelier with teardrops crystals dropping from the ceiling.

Mabel led Tonye and Laju into the sitting room.

The Persian rug was indeed magnificent. It was soft under his feet. *No wonder grandmother made such a fuss about it*, Tonye thought. He found it hard to believe that a seventy-something-year-old woman lived there. It was cosy and full of youthful life. There were four flowered armchairs and a curved sofa with velvet cushions. There were well-polished stools beside each chair and a small mahogany center table. The lighting was mild, coming from three chandeliers spread across the ceiling. The large dining area had a long table with hand-carved chairs on both sides and two huge grandiose chairs on each end.

This was indeed a 'living' room, Tonye thought. Grandmother had every right to be meticulous with it. Anyone would, especially someone her age.

Tonye and Laju settled on the sofa and waited for grandmother while they sipped the malt drinks Mabel had served them.

"How are you feeling?" Laju asked, smiling at her fiancé.

"Scared stiff," Tonye said.

"Come now, my darling. Everything will be alright," Laju said, taking Tonye's trembling hand.

"I don't know how many times I've said this, but your grandmother's house is beautiful," Tonye said.

"Thanks. My uncle, Richmond, designed and built it for her about five years ago."

"Oh. I see."

They were making small talk and laughing when Mabel rushed in.

"Mama don come, mama don come," she said, rushing to clear the bottles and their half-empty glasses. She wiped the surface of the stool with a cloth, replaced the stool to its former position, and disappeared. Tonye could imagine why she was acting that way. The falcon had come back to her nest.

The door to the living room swung open, and grandmother waltzed in with a smile on her face and her arms wide open.

Tonye and Laju both sprang to their feet.

"Oh, my baby, my darling golden girl. Come over here," grandmother said. Laju ran into grandmother's arms for a warm embrace.

"Hello, grandma," she said.

"How are you my dear? I heard you drove all the way from Lagos just to see me. Why didn't you fly?" grandmother said, taking a seat in one of the chairs.

"Tonye insisted on driving. Grandma, this is my fiancé, Tonye Kemefa," Laju said, gesturing at Tonye.

Grandmother looked up at him, her smile gone. She had not answered his earlier greetings, but Tonye took it that she must not have heard him since she had seemed so happy at the sight of her granddaughter.

"Oh. This is the Ijaw boy you spoke to us about. How are you, young man?" she said. Tonye felt naked under her cool gaze..

"I'm fine, ma. And you?" Tonye said, choosing his words with care.

"Well, what can an old woman like me do? I'm alright. Please do sit down," she said. Tonye obeyed.

"What a fine young man. Have you two had anything to drink? Mabel!" she called, without waiting for them to answer.

"Ma," the maid said as she ran in.

"Prepare my bath. I am in desperate need of a warm shower."

"Yes ma," the maid replied and disappeared again.

"Come my angel. Bring these bags to my room. We'll talk there," grandmother said, standing. She had such strength and agility.

"Yes grandma," Laju said, picking up grandma's bags.

"Young man, please make yourself comfortable. We'll be with you soon. You know the way we women talk," she said. She walked out of the living room, leaving Laju and Tonye alone for a moment.

"Honey just give us a second," Laju said, kissing him on his cheek.

"She hates me," Tonye said.

"Oh, no she does not. Remember what we talked about. No matter what, it's just you and me. Just the two of us, okay?"

"Didn't you see the look on the maid's face when you first told her my name? It was like you'd spoken a curse aloud or something."

"Baby, you're overreacting."

"And your grandmother slaughtered me with her eyes.

"Tonye…"

"Please, could you put on the TV for me before you leave?"

"Let me get Mabel to do that. Granny is waiting," she said, giving him one last kiss before slipping out of the living room.

Tonye didn't have to feel alone after Laju left. He *was* alone.

*

Grandmother regarded the two of them with piercing eyes through her gold-rimmed glasses. The look on her face said she had seen all the sorrows in the world. She shifted in her chair, maintaining her gaze while Laju spoke. Tonye wondered if she was listening to what her granddaughter was saying. She seemed to be in another world as she squeezed the chair arms.

Laju held Tonye's hand.

"Grandma, we love each other. How can you say you cannot give us your blessings to get married?" Tears rolled down her cheeks, but there was no other indication that she was crying.

"Laju, my dear, that is just how it is. Heavens, he is an Ijaw boy, for crying out loud," the old woman said. Her voice seemed to tremble. "I mean, who knows what *they* will do to you," she added.

"Madam, with all due respect," Tonye interrupted, unable to remain silent. "I believe the choice of a

19

husband is the girls to make, not her family's. Laju has made her choice, and I've made mine. We love each other and that's all that matters," Tonye said, fighting to control his temper.

"My son, I don't hate you, as you must think I do. I am just being realistic. I just cannot stand for it, not with all that has been going on between our people and the Ijaws as of late."

"Grandma, for heavens' sake! This is 1997, not the 1800s. You cannot destroy a perfect union just because of some silly ethnic rivalry between the Ijaws and the Itsekiris. Tonye is a fine man who can take loving care of me. Besides, my parents are already in consent of our marriage," Laju said in one breath.

"Oh? Your father agrees, huh? I see that Lagos has blinded that boy," grandmother said, picking up the telephone receiver from a stand beside her. Both Laju and Tonye hadn't seen that coming. They had not seen the telephone sitting right beside her.

The young couple was silent. Tonye wondered who the old lady was calling, but Laju looked as though she knew. Soon, it was obvious.

"Hello my dear, it's me. Oh, fine thank you. Is Dele at home? Okay. Tell him to call me as soon as he gets home. Yes dear. Bye," she replaced the receiver.

"Grandma, calling my father won't change anything," Laju said. She was angry, but she managed to remain composed.

"Someday, you'll understand that what I'm doing is for your own good."

"You know what, I think I'll go wait in the car," Tonye said as he stood up. He had to leave the room. Otherwise, he might have said something he would regret later. The old woman was still his future grandmother-in-law, despite the hatred he now felt for her. He was sure that the feeling was mutual. Nevertheless, he was determined to give her all the respect due her.

"Baby, I'm right behind you. Just give me thirty minutes," Laju said in a hushed voice. He nodded and turned to face Grandmother Dawson.

"It was such an honor to meet you, mama. You have a beautiful home," he said with a bow.

"Thank you my dear. Drive well," she said dryly.

Tonye walked out.

Outside Grandmother Dawson's mansion, Tonye decided to go for a stroll to clear his head. He needed to think. He needed to put things in perspective. Perhaps Grandmother Dawson was right. Maybe Laju's and his love wasn't meant to exist. He tried not to think of anything that could come between him and his fiancée, but he couldn't clear his mind of all the sudden negativity. He loved Laju more than life itself, and he wasn't going to let anything come between them, but somewhere in his heart, reality was beginning to sink in. If nobody gave their marriage a blessing, then what was the use marrying into the family? Was love all they needed? Was *their* love strong enough?

He saw a NITEL telephone booth and walked over to it. A man was making a call, and the entire world could hear his conversation, even though he was locked within the booth. Tonye reached in his back pocket for his wallet and produced two NITEL calling-cards.

What would life be without Laju? He couldn't bring himself to think of it.

Tonye had been a different man when he met Laju eighteen months ago, in a coffee shop in Notting Hill, England. She had been on holiday, away from her postgraduate school in East London. The moment he saw her from across the café, he knew she was Nigerian, and he just had to have her. What a stunning beauty she was!

"May I buy you another cup of coffee?" he had asked in Nigerian pidgin walking over to her table, interrupting her reading. She looked up at him with a strange look on her face, like she didn't have the slightest clue what he had said.

"I'm sorry, were you talking to me?" she had asked in fluent English. She had a somewhat British accent.

"I'm sorry. I thought you were someone else," he had said with a smile.

"Oh. Okay," she said, and went back to her book.

"Hope you don't mind me asking, are you a Nigerian?"

She looked up and smiled. "Yes, I am Nigerian."

"I thought as much. No wonder you looked just like my friend."

"Oh? What's her name?" Laju had asked. She could see the surprise on his face.

"Beg your pardon?"

"I asked for her name. Perhaps I might know her."

"Em… Angela," Tonye said, fidgeting.

"Angela. Hmmmm…let me see. Do I know her?" Laju said, trying to think. "Is she studying in Oxford or Birmingham?" she asked him.

Tonye sighed defeated.

"Ok, there's no Angela. I saw you from across the café and you looked so beautiful. I'm sorry if I embarrassed you," he said with a charming smile.

"I see. So, you were trying to trick me, right?" Laju had said, this time in Nigerian Pidgin. She was stifling a giggle.

"Please, pardon me. So, what are you reading?" Tonye said and offered himself a seat.

On that playful note, they had become friends. Before he met her, he was a regular Casanova. After that day in the café, she didn't try to change him. As their friendship grew, it was obvious that he was falling in love with her. He trusted her with everything. She knew about all his so-called relationships which always ended in disasters. One time he had dated a rich Nigerian princess from the ancient Benin City who happened to be a partner in the law firm where he worked. It didn't last and as usual, he dumped her. She went *Xena* on him. She destroyed his car, swore to kill him, and tried to get him fired. He was so close to a sexual-harassment lawsuit had Laju not hidden him in her apartment for a whole week. It was during that time Laju started seeing his better sides. But as usual he always went back to be the Casanova after the ass-saving, yet she was always there for him. After four months of being 'just friends,' Tonye surprised Laju by going down on his knees and begging her to look upon him. She had laughed and agreed to date him, but she made sure he had changed. And he had. Mr. Casanova became Mr. Right.

"Mr. Man, will you make a call or not?" The husky voice of one of the people waiting in line behind him to use the phone brought him back to reality.

"Oh. I'm sorry," he said and slid into the phone booth. He inserted the call card and dialled his parents' house in Lagos. His mother picked up.

"Mummy, it's not looking good," he said once he heard his mother's voice on the other side of the line.

*

Laju locked herself in the toilet of the guestroom and let herself slip to the ground. She needed to cry. How could they do that to her? After all the civility and exposure her family had, how could they be so uncivilized when she needed them to be most understanding and caring? She needed to cry for herself, a grown but helpless woman who needed the blessing of her family to move on with her life and marry the man she loved. How could she break away from this family? She knew she couldn't. She needed to cry for the love of her life, tears for Tonye Kemefa.

Laju wept for about half an hour before she washed her faced, repaired her make-up, and went to tell her grandmother that she was leaving.

As she left the Dawson mansion with Grandmother Dawson on her heel walking her to the door, she prayed Tonye was still waiting for her. She prayed to the high heavens that grandmother had not scared him away. She prayed with all the faith left in her that he still loved her and that he knew that this was just a hurdle they would have to jump over together.

Tonye was reading one of the dailies when she got to the car. He'd waited for two hours and twenty-seven minutes. His demeanour was as if nothing had happened in the Dawson mansion. He was calm and chivalric. It was something she had not seen before; something so wonderful that she fell in love with him all over again.

"Hey baby, how did it go in there with the old lady?" He asked folding the newspaper and starting the car engine as Laju slid into the passenger side.

"We're going to be just fine," she said.

Of course she wasn't going to tell him that after he had left her father had called back and after hearing her grandmother say, *"I don't want my granddaughter marrying some Ijaw boy"*, he had asked to speak with her and all he could say was, *"we'll talk about it when you return to Lagos."*

As Tonye drove Laju to her auntie's house where she was staying, thunder struck, and lightning flashed- it was going to rain.

Two.

Mogha and Seye

PAPERS SCATTERED EVERYWHERE, up-turned tables, picture frames pulled off walls, drawers yanked open, a lonesome briefcase in a corner; Jonah Aroromi could not figure out what he was looking for. Ever since his bosom friend called him three hours ago telling him that *they* were coming for him, he had been gathering essentials for his escape; pictures of his family, documents of the deeds to his houses and landed properties spread across the city, keys to his cars and of course the briefcase loaded with cash in US Dollars. He could not stop his heart from racing. He wondered why the Ijaw militia wanted him dead. It had to be his wealth because he could not think of any other reason. He'd never been a part of any sort of coalition and he sure wasn't planning on being a part of the ethnic war everyone knew was brewing. Preye didn't say when the militia was coming or why he was a target. It could be anytime. Hell, it could be now.

Jonah picked up the telephone receiver for the seventh time and again there was no dialling tone. His heart raced even faster. The last time he had spoken with his sons holidaying in the UK was three days ago, and from the way they sounded, he suspected they were planning to surprise him with their arrival. Yesterday he didn't have much to worry about, so he was looking forward to their arrival but today, he wanted his children as far away from the city as possible. He needed to make that one phone call.

He rushed upstairs to his bedroom, flung open the wardrobe doors and stared into its already torn-apart contents. Only the heavens could tell what was racing through his mind. He threw things out of the wardrobe to reveal a small secret vault forged into the wall with security combination buttons. He entered his security code and after a few seconds he pulled open the door of the vault. He brought out the contents and laid them on the bed. His international passport was one of the things in the vault. He slipped it into his back jeans pocket and left the room without giving second thoughts to the other contents of the vault or bothering to secure the vault again.

In the sitting room he picked up the phone, elated to hear a dialling tone. He dialled his daughter Serena's number in the UK. It began to ring.

"Hello, Serena. Thank goodness I could get through to you. I've been trying to reach you for about an hour now," he said, in one breath.

"Hello dad, are you alright? You don't sound well," Serena's indistinct voice replied.

"Serena, where are the boys?" he asked at once, the desperation clear in his voice.

"Well, they insisted on not telling you and I can

assure you I had nothing to do with it..." his daughter began, and he feared the worst.

"Not telling me what? What are you talking about?"

"Seems they are on their way to Warri as we speak. They left the UK two days ago."

"What!? On their way where? To Warri? Oh my God." Jonah held his chest as if preventing a heart attack from occurring.

"Daddy what's going on? Why are you so upset about their coming home? I mean, it was only meant to be a harmless surprise."

"Serena, the boys cannot come to Warri. I've packed up a few things and I'm leaving town right now."

Serena was silent as if to better understand what her father was talking about.

"Leaving town? Why? And how does that affect the boys?"

"Serena, an ethnic war has been brewing in the past few weeks between the Ijaws and Itsekiris and I've become a target," Jonah explained.

"What? Oh my God, a target? Dad, what are you talking about?"

"I'm saying an Ijaw militia could very well be on their way to come and kill me if I don't leave this town right now. And now you tell me my sons are coming here. What am I going to do?" he slumped into the chair next to him clutching the phone receiver to his ears as he felt his legs weaken.

"Dad, I'm scared. You need to get out of there. For all I know Mogha and Seye won't be in Warri for a couple of days more. I mean, they only just landed in Nigeria yesterday. The last time they called me, they were at Auntie Omagbemi's house in Lagos. They might still be there," Serena said. Jonah could tell she was crying. He was silent.

"But dad, you need to get out of there. I beg you, leave Warri. Daddy, abeg comot for dat town, I don't…"

"Hello, Serena you're breaking off. Hello…."

"I…. go…. too…. hear me?" those were the last words Jonah heard from his daughter before the line went dead. He hit the engage button in anger and listened, there was no dial tone. He slammed the receiver on the phone and pushed the phone away as hot tears gathered in his eyes.

What was he going to do? As much as he loved his sons with all his heart, he needed to make sure he was safe for their sake. Serena could be right. Maybe, his sons had not left Lagos yet. But the thought that Serena could be wrong broke his heart to tiny pieces.

His life flashed before his very eyes.

He remembered the day when Mogha was born like it was only yesterday. He'd promised his wife they wouldn't have another child after him. They already had three, Serena, Austin and Mogha, only to hear of her pregnancy just three years after practicing family planning. He couldn't be happier to welcome Seye into the pack and so did everyone else in the household with so much love and pampering.

He remembered his beautiful wife, Tola, who died seven years ago after battling a rare case of lung cancer. She never smoked once in her life. He wished she was there with him now. He wished she could see how well he had done holding the family together. He missed her so much. Somehow, she had always known what to do in any situation. He longed for her counsel.

No way was he going to let anything happen to his sons. He had to do something.

There was a series of loud knocks on the front door. His heart did a double flip as he expected the worse and at the same time hoped it was his sons.

The knock came again, and this time followed by a familiar voice. It was his friend Preye. He rushed to the door to let him in.

"What are you still doing here? I just thought I should come over and make sure you'd left, but here you are," Preye said rushing into the house and shutting the door behind him.

"I don't think I can leave. My sons are on their way here," Jonah said with sadness in his eyes.

"What? Your sons? Aren't they supposed to be in the UK?"

"Serena said they left the UK two days and that they might still be in Lagos at their auntie's, but she isn't sure. I can't make any calls. The lines are dead," Jonah said defeated.

"Well that is a possibility you should believe in. Besides, I'm ready to stay here for the rest of the day, should they show up."

Jonah was silent.

"You need to leave Jonah. Everyone is leaving. Did you hear that Chief Layemo Smith has also fled the city? I mean this is one of the foremost leaders of the Itsekiri Union."

"Well, I have no idea. In case you've forgotten, I do not belong to any stupid union and right now I have greater problems."

Preye was quiet.

"I'm sorry for my rudeness Preye. Thank you for all you've done. You are a faithful friend."

"Thank me when you and your family are safe and away from here. Now you need to go. I'll be here waiting for your sons."

"How did we get here?" Jonah wondered, as he prepared to flee from his own home. A home he'd shared with his family for more than two decades. It was sad. Even sadder to think that his sons might be walking right into a war zone and there was nothing he could do to stop them. Jonah looked out the window; it looked like it was going to rain.

*

Nine Hours Later.

Mogha and Seye's flight from Lagos landed before the rain started in the Warri Airport. However, for many passengers, most flights would either get delayed or cancelled. The brothers had just finished a three-month vacation in London with their eldest and only sister and were looking forward to one wonderful week with their father before returning to school.

Mogha was a twenty-one-year old youth with the features of a man. He had well-cut, and one would call him 'sir' when one saw his well-trimmed side burns and thick moustache. He was a handsome youth with so much of his father in him. He was strong and responsible and could carry on a conversation with an old lady like he understood the tales from her youthful days. His father always wondered why he was so mature given he wasn't his first son. Austin was mature but compared to Mogha, he wouldn't stand a chance. Mogha had a way of caring for the troubles of the world; little wonder he opted to be a medical doctor. He was caring and soft-hearted but with a lot of wisdom. His looks went a long way to help develop him into the young man he was, but no one could understand the configuration of Mogha Timilehin Aroromi.

A third-year medical student at the University of Benin, Mogha could not wait to get back to school even though he'd just had one of the best holidays in a long time. But the reality was that he had a marathon of reading to do for his forth coming MBBS exams.

"Hope you haven't called Dad since we landed in Lagos," Seye asked in his usual playful manner.

"No, I haven't. I thought we agreed it'd be nice to surprise him," Mogha replied giving directions to the taxi-driver.

"Yeah. I doubt if he'd be surprised anyway. Nothing

surprises that guy," Seye said.

"What do you mean he wouldn't be surprised?"

"Well, considering that Serena must've called to give him our itinerary, I would say nope, he wouldn't. Anyway, whatever. I'm hungry man."

"Just hang in there, buddy. We'll be home soon."

"Yeah, can't wait."

Seye, who was a first-year Law student in the same university as his older brother, was about three inches taller than Mogha. People sometimes mistook him to be the older one but the moment he talked, they knew at once otherwise. People walked on egg shells around him and let him to do whatever he wanted if he didn't hurt anyone. Their parents pampered them all from the beginning, but when their mother died seven years ago, everyone felt obligated to do everything to make sure their baby brother coped with the loss. Serena had taken up the role of mother and even after she got married and moved to England with her family, she'd always found a way to make sure her baby brothers still got the full doze of her magic wand of pampering.

It was raining pins and needles by the time Mogha and Seye's taxi pulled up in front of their house, found in one of the more developed and luxurious parts of Ugborikoko just a short drive from the miniature airport. By the time, the boys got their luggage from the trunk of the taxi, struggled with the huge gate, and rushed to the front porch, they were already drenched.

"Bollocks! What kind of rain is this? Why would it have to rain the day I came back home? And why isn't anyone opening the door?" Seye sulked.

"I don't see Dad's car; I think he's gone out." Mogha said looking out back to their father's parking space.

"Well, all our cars are out. That's strange," Mogha continued.

"Please bro, get us in the frigging house. Don't you have the keys anymore?" Seye asked, already shivering.

"Hey, watch the language lazy bones. Come, hold this," Mogha handed his rucksack to his brother while he sorted out the house key from a bunch of keys he had retrieved from his bag.

The boys could not believe what they saw when they entered the house. It was like a tornado had gone right through their living room. Everything was up-side-down. Nothing was in its usual place. And it sure didn't look like a remodelling had taken place while they were away.

"What do you think happened here?" Seye asked. The question was more rhetorical than meant for anyone.

The boys made their way into their home and as they went further into the house, they had more shocking discoveries awaiting them.

Seye picked up the phone; it was dead.

"Phone's dead," He shouted to his brother who was in another wing of the large house.

"So is everything else including the electricity. So much for surprising Dad," Mogha muttered the latter to himself.

The brothers climbed up the stairs, afraid of what they

could find. Their father's bedroom had even more surprises, including the fact that someone had compromised their father's secret vault.

"Jesus! It looks like we were robbed while Dad was away," Mogha said scavenging through his father's vault and wardrobe. "I don't know what was here before, so I can't tell what's missing."

"Where is Dad?" Seye asked another rhetorical question.

"I found something." Mogha said, bringing out a briefcase from inside the wardrobe.

Seye joined his brother and they opened the briefcase. They found it strange that the case had no lock engaged, because cash, in US dollars, filled it.

"Jesus! What the…"

"Wait. There's something else," Mogha said as he noticed that there was a note taped to the inside of the lid of the briefcase. It read, 'LOOK UNDER THE BED.'

The boys regarded each other for a quick second and rushed to their father's bedside falling over each other. Seye was the first to sight the white envelope under the bed. He stretched under and retrieved it. The boys regarded the familiar handwriting on the envelope and fear began to set in.

"What's happening?" Mogha said. He knew his brother was trying to be brave, but he needed to be brave for them.

They sat on their father's bed and opened the

envelope.

Reality awakened from a deep slumber.

*

Nine Hours Earlier.

The dark clouds of rain began to clear up as quickly as they'd first appeared, and Jonah felt a little hope rise in him. Maybe, Serena was right. Maybe his sons didn't set for Warri when they got into Nigeria. His friend Preye had left a few minutes ago and promised to get back as soon as he could find a safe place to move his cars to. There were six cars in all in his compound and three belonged to his sons. Austin was away in the United States doing his post-graduate studies but whenever he came home, he always had a car at his disposal. The other three were Jonah's. He had spent a lot of money buying and maintaining the cars but suddenly they all seemed like burdens to him now. All he was concerned about was the safety of his sons. He was confused, detached from his normal mental state and it was in this state that he did something that he hoped would save his children's lives.

Ready to leave, Jonah picked up the briefcase and rushed back upstairs to his bedroom. He got out his writing pad and began to write a painful letter to his sons with certain instructions should they come home while he was away. He finished and put it in a white envelope. He looked around the room for the best place to keep it for them. An idea struck him. He slipped it under the bed and tore out another sheet from his pad. He scribbled the words 'look under the bed' on the paper, opened the briefcase loaded with cash and stuck the paper inside the lid. He closed the case making sure he didn't use the combinations, so anyone could open them and placed the two briefcases inside his wardrobe using just a few of his clothes to conceal them. He knew if his sons got home and saw the house scattered like that, they would follow the trail to his bedroom and in no time discover the money and the letter. But in all this, he prayed that his sons never get there. He preferred a total stranger have his hands on the money than for his sons to face such danger. The money meant nothing to him at that moment.

A few minutes later Preye returned and Jonah handed him the keys to his house and five of his cars. There was no looking back now.

"Please be careful Preye, you put yourself at risk just by helping me," Jonah said as he got into one of the cars.

"It's alright. You take care. As soon as I'm done parking the cars I'll come and keep a look out for your sons. But I pray they don't show up."

"I pray so more than you know. For all we know this could just blow over and be just another false alarm, the crisis I mean," Jonah said as he started the car engine.

"God speed, my dear friend," Preye waved as Jonah drove off.

Jonah did not look back as he drove away from a life he'd known forever. His company headquarters was in Abuja, but a substantial amount of his revenue came from Warri. Leaving now, like this, meant he was taking himself away from his business. He prayed for his children, and for peace in Warri and more than anything he prayed that this crisis turned out to be just a mere quarrel between a handful of youths. But as Jonah left the city behind, he could see a cloud of smoke rising from a far distance into the sky. He wondered if it was a bonfire or what. He thought of his children; of his business; of his friends and allies. Were they all running like he was or were they standing to fight? He was being a coward. Maybe, he jumped the gun. Whatever it was, he was glad to breathe the air as he drove to the ancient city of Benin.

Three.

Toritseju and Jolomi

"WHY WOULDN'T YOU LOOK AT ME? Why wouldn't you say something?" Jolomi said, pleading to his wife.

Toju didn't turn around from the window. She didn't want her husband to see the tears already welling up in her eyes. She wished the pain would cease. She wished it would just go away, far away from her, so she could live again. Outside their apartment it had just started to rain. It was just another typical rainy day in Warri. Soon the whole compound would flood. Alas, the whole city would soon be an ocean, and she would begin to bail rivers of water from her living room floor. She had a lot of work to do. She didn't need Jolomi talking about his 'causes.' She didn't need the words of her husband to drown away what she wanted to hear around her. All she needed was a little bit of peace and quiet, if only for just a few minutes. She didn't believe in the world anymore, anyway.

"What do you want me to say, Jolomi?" Toju replied, still not turning from the window. It was as if she could see a certain beauty outside in the city that no else could see. Luckily for them, their apartment was the first one in the compound, so she could see a part of the neighborhood. As for others, it was plain face-me-I-face-you. What hope could she see in this town? She had always asked herself that question ever since she had arrived here for which she could not think of an answer.

"Toritseju, my love," Jolomi was standing behind her now. She could feel his breath on the nape of her neck. Her heart skipped a beat. She wanted to smile but there was none left inside of her. She turned to face him without saying a word.

"Toju, you know I love you. I love you more than anything in this world and you know I would never do anything to put this family in danger. But this is something I must do," he spoke to her with his eyes searching hers. She once had so many things written in her eyes, things you could read. But now, not so much, only pain.

"Something you have to do? Something you have to do, huh, Jolomi"? She slipped away from him and went to sit on what looked like a chair but had lost all the 'chair' essentials. At least it still stood on four wooden legs with thin foam covering the wood; the cloth used in wrapping it had since lost any hope of survival. The chair itself was begging to die. A slight chill was getting the best of Toju's feet. She folded her legs on the chair and wrapped her arms around them as she gave a loud sigh, a sign for Jolomi to say no more.

What did he think he was getting himself into? Did he think this was a game of 'police and thief' children play

40

every day? This was war and he was choosing to be a part of it even now that it may only well be just beginning.

"Jolomi, can you tell me again what you could do to stop two ethnic groups from going head-to-head with each other? Something which has been recurring for years."

"So many things, Toju, so many things. This is what I trained to do, remember? Just as you play your part every day in the hospital, so I must play my part as a journalist," Jolomi said squatting in front of his wife.

"Play my part in the hospital? If only you knew what I see there every day. The pain, the horror, and just maybe you would know that I'm not playing a role at all. Rather, I'm trying to mend what's left. Sometimes I just want to run away."

"But we can't. This is our people. This is our fight."

"Your fight? Jolomi it's only just beginning. The family living three apartments away from us doesn't even know yet that there's a war going on. We are privileged to know because I am a doctor and I treat burnt victims who come in everyday from remote Ijaw and Itsekiri villages and hear their gory stories. And you dare call it *your* fight? How dare you!" Toju said putting her leg back on the ground. "Look out there Jolomi, just take a good look. Does it look like Warri knows what's coming?" she finished. It was like she needed to root her feet to the ground to enable her say that much.

"I understand, but I am a seasoned journalist. Jesus Christ Toju! We both went to some of the best schools in the world for heaven's sake. In what better way can we put our education to use if not to educate our people about this war?"

"And tell them what J? We have already sacrificed everything. Look at where we live. I'm not one to complain, you know me. I chose to come here on my own and I am grateful that you followed me all the way but let's enjoy the peace while we still have it. You don't need to be on the warfront covering the news." There were a thousand and one pleadings in her eyes.

"See, this job I'm taking doesn't mean I'll be thrown to the war zone. Besides we wouldn't call it war. It's just a bunch of boys with guns."

"Oh Lord! Jolomi, I know you and your causes. Do you remember Rwanda? I mean it has only been two years. I almost died in New York waiting for you to come back. And when you did come back you came back a near-dead man. I fear that person in you would re-emerge the moment you accept Chief Warebi's offer."

"Come on T. My job is no different from what you do. How long have we been in Warri?"

"About ten months."

"Ten months, huh. And how many times have your father and mine sent us cars to help us leave?"

Toju managed a smile.

"Too many times," she said.

"And we are still here. Aren't we?" Jolomi said in a whisper.

Toju was silent.

"I agreed to work with Chief Warebi because we believe in the same cause," Jolomi added.

"But he is an Ijaw chief. The one considered a patriarch to the Ijaw people. What do you think will happen when people find out?" The worry took over Toju's face.

"I am a journalist T. I represent the truth and people deserve to know. The world needs to know what's going on, and right now no one seems to be saying anything about it. Chief Warebi knows people and with his help we can let the world know. It's all for peace my darling wife," he said in a bid to cheer her up.

"Don't 'darling' me. We still need to know what measures the chief is taking to guarantee your safety."

"Mine and yours. *Our* safety," Jolomi said and kissed her on her forehead.

Toju heaved a sigh.

"Jolomi, we have so much to lose. I don't want to lose you. Not again."

"I know. You won't lose me. This is not Rwanda." Jolomi opened his arms and she went into his embrace.

Toritseju closed her eyes and began to remember things. Things she had tried to bury deep in her mind. Things she had seen and things she had lost. She remembered how things used to be and what things had become now.

*

Jolomi felt a jab in his chest as he felt his very delicate but strong heart pound even faster. As he held his wife in his bosom, he knew she was deep in thoughts and so was he. He could feel her heart beat against his chest and her warm breath seemed to be caressing the long horizontal scar hidden underneath his chest hairs. The scar told the story of his life with Toju. But he didn't want to go there. Not now; not right now. Perhaps Toju was right. He was in over his head and he needed to take things slow. He didn't want to put her through what she experienced while he was in Rwanda all over again. But he knew he was doing the right thing. This wasn't a matter of rumours. He'd seen first-hand what war was all about, and so had Toju. If nothing happened to let people know what was going on in the creeks of the Delta, in a week, or even a few days, there would be nothing left of the city and he could not have that on his conscience. He wished he could satisfy his wife this one time; he wished they could just park up and run, but that was not what he was all about, and neither was she. They were both fighters and it took only him to acknowledge that fact. He loved her so much and he didn't want to lose her, but as much as she meant the world to him, so did telling the truth.

Chief Warebi's offer was hard to resist. He would get to do what he loved and be a part of something great. A revolution! That was what the Ijaw chieftain had called it and that was too much of an offer to pass up. Toju wouldn't understand what this meant to him. He thought she would be glad he was a vital part of what was to come, just as she played a significant role in a hospital that treats 'everyone' irrespective of their ethnic

44

background. He couldn't blame her. She'd been through a lot in the past two years, ever since he came into her life - and he wished there was something he could do to change the past. But the past was gone, and they could only look toward the future. He was determined to make sure their future become greater than their past, which hadn't been.

His wife released herself from his embrace and walked into their bedroom without saying another word. It still rained outside and Jolomi wondered when it would stop. He was supposed to meet with Chief Warebi today and he didn't want to miss the meeting.

He slumped into a chair and closed his eyes.

Things used to be great in their home. Things used to be perfect in their home. The home he shared with the woman who once saved his life and the woman who loved him enough to marry him despite all that hung around him.

Flashes of lightning penetrated his closed eyelids and he knew that a clap of thunder would follow, but he did not open his eyes. Instead he let that blind tranquillity led him into a world he knew would be hard to forget.

*

"The central portion of Rwanda is dominated by a plateau averaging about one thousand seven hundred meters, that's about five thousand six hundred feet in elevation," Naigiziki, the young British-born Rwandan journalist intern assigned to accompany Jolomi from London to Rwanda, said.

Jolomi smiled and continued writing in his notebook

while Rwandan chattered on about his home country. He must have read all the stuff that came out of his mouth from an Encyclopedia or something because he was just as new a visitor to Rwanda as Jolomi himself was. With his polished English accent and excited looks, one could tell how eager he was to go meet his ancestral plains.

"Eastward, toward the Tanzanian border, the land slopes downward to a series of marshy lakes along the upper Kagera River," he continued wide-eyed.

Jolomi looked out the window of the chatter plane. On the western side of the plateau was a mountain system forming the watershed between the Nile and Congo River systems. The Virunga Mountains had a volcanic range that formed the northern reaches of this system which included Volcan Karisimbi, Rwanda's highest peak. West of the mountains, the elevation dropped into the Lake Kivu region. The self-proclaimed tour-guide Naigiziki pointed out all these.

Jolomi massaged the huge horizontal scar on his chest as he let his mind fill with thoughts of his new wife back in New York. A smile lingered on his face. He jolted back to reality as the chatter plane touched down on the Kigali International Airport.

It was April 1995, one year after the Rwandan Civil War, which was genocide during which between five hundred thousand and one million Rwandans, like Tutsi, were massacred. As he and his young intern climbed down the plane, and as Jolomi took in the air that was Rwanda, his stomach cringed. It was as if he could still smell the stench of death, remnant from the massacres of April 1994. He looked at his intern; the young man was smiling and taking pictures with his disposable camera. How could he not feel anything that Jolomi was feeling? How could he be a Rwandan and yet not react to what went on here only a year ago? For a minute there, Jolomi wished he could be as carefree as Naigiziki was.

It didn't take them long to get a taxi that would take them to Jolomi's contact Pierre, a Tutsi.

Naigiziki went on taking pictures amidst his regular tour-guide tips while Jolomi did all the thinking. Pierre had told him to be careful when coming to Rwanda. Though it was a year since the genocide, he'd warned, things weren't yet peaceful. So, while Naigiziki went on about this place and that place –Jolomi didn't see anything worth chatting about, all he could see was a land deserted and a place that people were afraid to call home again – Jolomi thought of their safety.

The taxi brought them to a market in Butare, a small urban center south of Kigali.

"Ziki, do you know how to work the map?" Jolomi said to his intern with a stern face. The young man stopped talking and shook his head.

"I didn't think so," Jolomi muttered under his breath. "First we'll need to get to a phone. I need to call my contact. I don't suppose they included these markets in the books you've been reading about sweet-home Rwanda, did they?" Jolomi teased managing a smile.

Naigiziki smiled back and scratched his head without replying.

Jolomi led the way as they made their way through the market which was quite busy and cheerful, not to

47

mention filthy given what they all had gone through in the past year. Well, like they say, happiness is the best cure to sadness. 'Whoever said that?' Jolomi wondered.

After the phone call, Jolomi and Naigiziki waited for Pierre in a stall where a woman cooked and sold sweet potatoes and beans served hot from a pot that looked like someone uprooted it from one of the war-torn, armored-tank ridden towns of the second World War. There were bottles of beer on every table the foreign journalists looked. As hungry as they were, they dared not request for a plate of the steamy-hot sweet potatoes and beans which seemed to be on everyone else's table except theirs. Jolomi looked over at Ziki; his eyes were hungry for his homeland delicacy.

"Why don't you try some? At least for your journal or travelogue or whatever it is you would write when you get back to England," Jolomi said, hoping the young chap would say no. He was surprised when Ziki agreed to his suggestion and ordered a plate. Good thing he could speak fluent French, since that was the language of communication. Jolomi looked on as the experimental journalist ate the food with a wince on his face after every bite.

"Mr. Benson?" Pierre's familiar voice called out after what seemed like an hour of waiting. Ziki was already dozing beside Jolomi.

"Yes," Jolomi said, standing up to meet the man as he walked up to him in the stall.

"My name is Pierre. It's an honor to put a face to your voice," Pierre's French accent was very distinct.

Jolomi smiled and took the man's firm handshake.

"The pleasure is all mine."

He turned to Ziki who seemed to have returned to England in his dreams and tapped him on the shoulder. The young man jumped.

"Let's get a move on, shall we?" Jolomi said as Ziki stood up and shook hands with Pierre.

"Now, let me show you my Rwanda," Pierre said with a smile. On his face Jolomi could see, amidst the smile, a lingering sadness that had a lot of stories to it.

The two strangers began to follow the man who knew the way.

Four.

Oyinmiebi

OYINMIEBI WAS BORED. Bored of everything; of the routine of waking up every morning and doing the very same thing he had done the day before and the day before that. He tired of being the perfect gentleman that everyone thought he was because he was a *seasoned* Law student. He needed more. He needed more to keep his adrenaline pumping. And he seemed to be looking for *more* everywhere he went. It'd been five years since he started studying Law and in one week, he would be writing his final exams and be through with the rigors of university life. He wondered what would be next. He was sure of more routine in Law school, but after that, what next? Charge and bail? He didn't think so. He needed more from life. He needed to take charge but for some reason he could not explain, he just could not take control of his life. Everything that had happened to him seemed to have occurred at a time when he had had no choice or say in the matter whatsoever. Even his choice of study was inflicted upon him by his father who believed that he needed a lawyer in the family to help solve all the 'land matters.' He was tired of people pushing him. He was tired of the *status quo,* but he had no idea how to turn things around.

Oyinmiebi, it is over. Please move on with your life and leave me alone. The words kept on replaying themselves in his mind as he packed his bags three weeks after he sent the final draft of his undergraduate thesis and prepared to bid farewell to university life. Whatever did he do to her to deserve such a rapid dismissal after three years? He could not put a finger on any reason at all. He'd been faithful to her, he'd supported her with the little that he had. He'd been there when she needed someone to trust. He'd given her the love that she deserved. She had meant the world to him, and he didn't hide that fact from her. How could she have been so cruel? It was stupid now to say he was going to win her back. They had been apart for months.

He picked up his Law of Torts textbook and stared at it for a minute before he flung it into the *Ghana-must-go* sack bag, in which he stored all his books. He could not believe he'd spent five years of his life doing something he had no passion for. That angered him.

His last visit home to Warri had been an eye-opener. His father had told him about a terrible problem the Ijaws were facing: the Itsekiris were trying to claim Warri as their own. Of course, Oyinmiebi had grown up knowing the history of bad blood between the Ijaws and the Itsekiris. He was also aware of all the stories and myths and legends of who was the *rightful* owner of the city. He had read about different accounts from each ethnic group of how the other ethnic group came to

51

settle in the city. Everyone in Warri knew the stories, and it was getting boring anyway. But this time his father spoke of things that were very worrisome to him. The old man believed that someone should 'teach those *land-thieves* a lesson they would never forget.' He spoke of anger and hatred and that scared Oyinmiebi.

It was in that spirit that Oyinmiebi, on his arrival, dropped his bags and left for the Ogbe-Ijoh waterside to see Zuokumo, his beloved cousin.

"Mama, *keide o*. I'm on my knees," Oyinmiebi greeted his Auntie as he entered the little house.

"Ah, *seri*. Stand up my son. How are you? It's been long since we last saw you. How's school?" the middle-aged woman, looking way older than she was, asked standing up from the fish she was smoking by the fireplace.

"Mama I don finish o. I'm through with school."

"Eeee. Thank God. You see am? God don do well for you o. School na power," she said throwing her hands into the air in jubilation as she broke into a song and dance.

Oyinmiebi smiled in embarrassment as Mama began to sing one of Robert Ebizimor's popular songs while she swayed her waist in the Ijaw *pingi* dance.

"Mama abeg where is Zuokumo?" he asked after Mama's little performance.

"At this time, he should be at the waterside?"

"Ok. I should just go and check there."

"Please make sure you come back before you leave. Let me start preparing some *kekefiia* for you."

"Ah mama, don't worry yourself."

"Oh, shut up. My son, you just finished school and you say I shouldn't worry. I wan use this dry *aloma* cook am."

"Okay mama," Oyinmiebi laughed, "I'll come back."

"Eeee. My *oyinbo* pikin. See as he dey speak well," Oyinmiebi overheard her say with pride and joy as he made his way out and headed for the riverbanks.

As he approached the river, he could see his cousin in a canoe throwing his fishing net into the water. He imagined his muscles flexing as he began to drag the water with the fishing net. His dexterity showed how well he knew what he was doing. It was as if the water responded to his demands and released the fish into his net because, by the time he pulled the last of the net onto his canoe, Oyinmiebi could see the number of fishes it had caught. He waited by the riverbank and watched his cousin work for a while without letting him know he was there.

Oyinmiebi looked up towards the sky as it began to darken. There was a trace of the sun behind the assembling rain clouds. He wished it wouldn't rain so he could spend some more time with his cousin out there by the riverbank.

Oyinmiebi admired the struggle of his people. He looked from one end of the shore to the other, the boats and canoes anchored there were enough to make up a fleet of warships. Those were their means of livelihood and they would do anything to protect them. He saw women, men, girls, and boys going on and coming off different canoes with their nets of different shapes and sizes. Fishing was not the only thing these people could do, but when they did, they did it with all their heart and soul.

That river bank meant a lot to the Ogbe-Ijoh people and especially to Oyinmiebi. He remembered, when growing up, he used to go fishing with his father on this very river. He would climb onto the boat with him and help him in untangling the fish that caught in the net. That time, so long ago, Oyinmiebi had wanted nothing more but to grow up and become a fisherman just like his father.

Back then, things were different. Magical.

By the riverbank, he and the other children in the vicinity would gather around a bonfire at night and would listen to stories of adventures from yonder years when men were boys and women were the girls they chased around. He would lie on his back on the sandy shore when he was tired of listening to story after story and would begin to count the stars. Each star he saw meant something to him. He would dream of becoming the greatest fisherman ever to live on the surface of the earth. He would imagine that he could communicate with the great god of the sea who gave the fish to the fishermen. He would dream of being an emissary to the gods and yet a great fisherman. He would lie back and dream dreams that even now he didn't know were possible.

By the riverbank he and his friends escaped to a world

of their own. A world each child created to fit his desires, and then they would share their imaginations with the others. Things were different back then.

And then there was Faith.

Oyinmiebi was thirteen years old when his crush on Faith started. Faith was the most beautiful girl to walk the plains of the earth. She was tall and had lanky legs that went on forever. He was just over ten years old then when his crush started and that was when he started feeling funny sensations between his thighs. Before that phase he always thought one could get an erection only in the morning when all the water his body had rejected gathered around his loins. He never knew he could get hard by just seeing Faith appear from the corner.

Faith was the daughter of a local chemist who had big dreams for his daughter, and so when she turned sixteen and was through with her secondary school education, he had sent her to her relatives in Lagos. Two years later she got a scholarship to study medicine in the university there and that was when she became the ideal child for every parent. If you didn't get a simple fisherman's equation right, your father would say, "Why can't you be like Faith and make something good out of your life?" If you refused to go on an errand, your mother would scream, "Oh, if only Faith were my daughter, I would not be stuck here with such a fool for a child."

By the riverbank Oyinmiebi dreamed of marrying the local beauty and showing her off around the world. Those days were golden; those days were magical, but those days were long gone. Boys had grown up to become men and most of the dreams never became reality. A lot of them did though; most of them became great fishermen.

Oyinmiebi smiled as he journeyed into the past. Reminiscence of days long gone but of memories so sweet. He heard a slight crackle of thunder as a soft, cool breeze whispered into his ears. He shivered and hugged himself as the cold crawled down his spine. Goose pimples stood on his skin. He looked out to his cousin whose hefty masculine body was unflinching even in the cold. He rocked the boat under his feet as he threw his net once again into the river. His back was to Oyinmiebi, so he had not noticed him yet. Oyinmiebi could see his muscles flex this time as he repeated his fisherman's routine. Here was a fisherman whom a young, university-trained lawyer-in-making admired.

Zuokumo who was older than Oyinmiebi had been the older brother he never had. Despite the huge education gap, the two always bonded. They always had something to talk about. Oyinmiebi never brought up issues that he knew would be too intellectual for his older cousin to discuss, and Zuokumo on his part never undermined his cousin's education. They were a duo. Whenever Oyinmiebi was away from home, he longed to get back just because he knew Zuokumo would have stories awaiting his return. Zuokumo was his eyes and ears when it came to matters affecting the community. He knew that, no matter what, he would know for sure about any forming plans.

A thunder clap again and Oyinmiebi felt it was time to announce his presence. By this time, the sun had been snuffed by the vicious rain clouds and Oyinmiebi felt a drop of rain land on his forehead and trickle down his face.

He looked over at his cousin and was relieved to see that he had pulled his net unto his canoe and was holding the paddle. Zuokumo still had his back to him.

"Hey bro," Oyinmiebi called out and his cousin turned. He waved at him and Oyinmiebi could see his face light up as he waved back and began to paddle towards shore.

"When did you get back, boy?" Zuokumo asked when Oyinmiebi went to join him as he pulled his canoe onto the sandbank.

"A few hours ago. And how is work?"

"My brother we dey manage. O boy, you be big boy now o. You don graduate abi?" Zuokumo teased his cousin as he tied his boat to a wood stuck at the riverbank.

"Well, something like that, but results never come out so I don't know yet."

"Anyway, I believe say you make am. You don reach our house? Have you been home already?" Zuokumo began to gather his net.

"Yes o. Mama don even begin preparing *kekefiia* for me sef," Oyinmiebi moved to help his cousin.

"Small o make you no stain yourself. Leave the net, I go carry am, but you go need wheelbarrow if you wan carry the fish o," Zuokumo said.

"Okay, where wheelbarrow dey na?" Oyinmiebi was

already rolling up his sleeves.

Zuokumo supplied a wheelbarrow from a corner and helped Oyinmiebi lift the basin of fish unto it.

As the young men walked back home, Oyinmiebi decided it was time for his updates.

"Okay Zuokumo, tell me, what is going on? My dad told me some things that have been worrying me," Oyinmiebi asked as they approached the house.

Zuokumo remained silent. He kept moving as if he did not hear what his cousin had just said.

Oyinmiebi opened his mouth to speak again but this time his cousin cut him short.

"Not now Oyinmiebi. I will give you the full gist later. But not now. Make we go chop for house. Let's go home and eat first," Zuokumo said, with a straight face without turning to look at Oyinmiebi.

Oyinmiebi remained silent and returned to pushing the wheelbarrow. He wondered why his cousin was acting strange. Maybe, he didn't want to let him in on what was going on. But why? Why would Zuokumo keep things from him? Whatever the cause, something big must be going on and if Zuokumo didn't tell him, he would find out himself.

They got home, and Oyinmiebi watched in silence as Zuokumo fastened his fishing net behind the house and overturned his catch into a bigger basin, so they could sort out the ones still alive from the dead ones.

"Una don come? Ah see the plenty fish wen you catch Zuokumo. You try o," Mama said joining them out back.

The boys greeted the woman. She announced that food was ready and retreated into the house as fast as she had appeared. Oyinmiebi decided to hold his peace and be patient until they had eaten. If Zuokumo still didn't say anything, he would confront him and demand why he was keeping whatever was happening from him.

That evening they ate in silence for the first time. Oyinmiebi had never eaten in silence with his beloved cousin before. Then why now, this evening, when the delicacy, starch and *kekefiia*, was more delicious than ever? They always had something to say. They never learned table manners, so talking while eating wasn't an issue in the household. They always had one thing or another to talk about while eating. If Oyinmiebi joined them for breakfast, they would talk about what they were expecting from the day; if he joined them for lunch, they would eat outside and talk about the girls that made *yanga* past them with their 'small *yansh* and pimpled breasts'; if he joined them for dinner, they would hear Mama complain about the woman next to her stall in the market and how wild she was and how the said woman's husband needs to teach her to respect her elders. There was always something to talk about during every meal.

But that evening they were silent. Even mama didn't say anything. Oyinmiebi wondered if she too knew something that he didn't. Of course, she could. She'd been in Warri all the while he'd been away. Everyone in Warri knew something that he didn't know. Why was he in the dark?

It had begun to rain outside now and one of the younger children in the house had gone to place

59

containers outside to catch some rain water and close the windows and doors.

After eating and thanking his Auntie for the meal, Oyinmiebi went to sit by the window and watch the rain fall. The pitter-patter of the rain on the roof was like music to his ears but not enough to soothe him from his absentmindedness. He looked out into the dim sky and wondered what went on up there. Who was Zeus battling with that he was throwing flashes of lightning every now and again? He smiled and shook the thought from his mind. Those were the very same theories he used to share with his friends while growing up, every time they played under the rain and saw a flash of lightning and heard a crack of thunder. When they were kids, there was always an explanation for everything. What made the rain fall, why pepper was peppery; why onions brought one to tears, why one digs a hole by the riverbank and finds water inside. Some of these theories made little sense now but most of them were just stupid but brought about so much fun to them. They had so much to live for when they were little children, but now Oyinmiebi didn't think so anymore.

"See, as you sit down for here by yourself as if sey person die. Why are you so gloomy, as if you are mourning the death of a loved one?" Zuokumo's voice jolted him back to the present.

Oyinmiebi sighed.

"Nothing bro. Just taking a journey down the memory lane," Oyinmiebi said turning to face his cousin who was now standing beside him.

"You know why I didn't say anything on our way home?" Zuokumo began.

Oyinmiebi remained silent and he continued.

"It's because you don't discuss such matters on the road. You never can tell who is listening in on your conversations."

"So, what's going on?" Oyinmiebi's resolve was stronger now.

"A lot of things are happening, my brother. These Itsekiri people will not allow us even a little peace of mind because they think they are the most educated of the bunch. You heard about the creation of the new Local Government, right?"

"Yes. Warri South-West local government area. What about it?" Oyinmiebi still could not understand where his cousin was leading to.

"Well, we had been made to believe that the headquarters of the new local government would be in Ogbe-Ijoh. But as we speak, we have heard strong rumours that the headquarters have been moved to Ogidigben."

"What?" Oyinmiebi was shocked. How could that be possible? And how could the news have missed him while he was in school?

"The Itsekiris are at work. We have heard concrete rumours that they will soon announce the creation of a Warri South-West local government area with headquarters in Ogbe-Ijoh, and now again we are hearing it has been changed to Ogidigben."

"It can't be."

"And there the Itsekiris are celebrating yet another victory."

"These people are pushing us too far," Oyinmiebi said. The anger was audible in his voice.

"And we will do something about it, you just wait and see. It's just a matter of time. We will," Zuokumo said in pure hatred.

"My father told me an Itsekiri man's house burned down, and that they are suspecting that Ijaw youths did it. Is it true?"

"I heard about that. But I don't know for sure. Do you know Chief Arimiebilador Oweila?" Zuokumo asked looking at his cousin straight in the eyes.

"Isn't he that billionaire who owns a lot of companies around Nigeria?"

"Yes. That one."

"What about him? Don't tell me he's been killed," Oyinmiebi asked.

"No. He's fine. We have a meeting with him next week."

"'We'? You and who?"

"Me. You. And about five hundred other able-bodied Ogbe-Ijoh youths."

"What will the meeting be about?" Now Oyinmiebi was beginning to sound naïve and stupid and when his cousin didn't answer his question, he wished he hadn't asked at all.

Oyinmiebi remained silent while his cousin told him some things to expect if the meeting with Chief Oweila went well. By the time he was going back home, his ears were full from all that his cousin had told him and funny enough he felt as if, for the first time in his life, his adrenaline had begun to pump - but then again, he wished it didn't pump too fast.

Dear Diary,

I never thought that in my lifetime, I would ever see a dead body from close view. But yesterday I did. Not one, but three. I should have entered these details yesterday, but I have been too shocked to even pick up my pen to write anything. I wonder when this war will stop. Warri used to be peaceful.

Life left Warri this year. She packed all her bags and left town and she wasn't looking back. Then death took over. The streets of Warri used to brim with life, so much merrymaking and jollity, more than one could experience in one day. The alleyways or 'corner-corner' of Ugborikoko used to teem with so many goings-on. Love and harmony flowed amongst the people. From the street ruffians to the low-lifers to whom life didn't seem so low. Market women at Okere, Poloko and Igbudu markets used to have better things to gossip about. They talked of the return of Onome from her daughter's house in Lagos. Onome had gone there to do' omuguo' after the birth of her first grandchild but she ended up overstaying her welcome. She had to be begged to return to her wares awaiting her in the market. They talked about Ebiere's husband who was sleeping with every young girl in town but Ebiere herself didn't seem to care. They talked about the death of Roli's father and after sharing their 'oohs' and 'aahs' they decided what best to wear for the funeral. Warri women! Warri life!

Warri was home to everyone until that dark Wednesday in 1997.

People were safe here. Just another town in the Niger Delta it was, but things have changed. It was destiny. Or maybe it was due to the workings and machinations of greedy and selfish humans that brought about the war. War came, all the same.

People used to have jokes to tell in Warri. Humour was the air the town breathed but when life left, the joke would be on the man whose life would end tomorrow or turn up on the wrong side of the town.

There were so many people living together in one place and so little trouble for the troublemaker to cook up. Life left Warri when sons killed fathers and looked at life as the enemy. Warri is desolate as boys became men overnight and took up arms to fight a war that should not have happened in the first place. Who knew that a city so pure, so free, so hopeful would overturn to ruins? The city weeps. Aye! We all weep for our city. Our beloved home.

The March rains of 1997 came faster than the year before. Everyone knew what to expect when it rained in Warri anyway, so it was business as usual. In Okumagba Layout, mothers called in their playing children as the clouds began to gather while fathers requested for the last of the 'ogogoro' in Mama Akporieme's shop. In Okere Market, women began to cover their wares with rubber bags: no one was parking just because it was about to rain, it was business as usual. In Ugborikoko everyone retired into their homes as the first of the rain drops hit the ground. Soon there would be many rivers to cross. Such was the life in Warri, and it was beautiful.

When it rained in Warri, it was as if the heavens opened its river banks and let the water flow into the city. What used to be a motor road became the River Ethiope. And it was beautiful.

When it rained in Warri, cars became canoes and the drivers became expert river-dwellers working their way through the waves.

And it was a remarkable sight still.

When it rained in Warri...oh, don't go outside, because you'd have to put away whatever pride you have and swim like everybody else. And it was beautiful, especially when you were watching from the safety of your house.

But the rains of 1997 didn't seem to bring any such joy. It didn't seem to bring with it, its usual tidings of hope, or love, or beauty, or fun. Neither did it seem to accept the laughter of children playing 'catch the raindrops' under the rain. Instead it came to flood the city. To take away the life it had. To stoke rather than extinguish the fires.

During the early parts of March, people around the city had heard of ethnic conflicts between the Ijaws and Itsekiris in the outskirts of the city, but no one ever saw anything. They'd heard of car burnings, of houses razed to the ground by mysterious fires, of deaths and sudden disappearances of key figures from both ethnic groups, but it was only in the news, and such stories were never confirmed by the people. Nothing seemed to happen in the mainland of Warri and so everyone went on with their businesses. It was business as usual.

And it was business as usual for me too when I carried my market basket, called upon my humble driver, and asked him to take me to Okere market. I felt it was time for me to cook my native Ewedu and Amala. But what awaited me at Okere market was something else. Oh, I wish I could forget but I can't. The horror.

Five.

Tonye and Laju

Tonye sat alone in his old bedroom on the second floor of his father's three-story house in the Poloko Market neighborhood of Warri. It had been a long while since they were in that house. It used to be their regular holiday hub before they all grew up and stopped visiting together with their parents. Now the house was just empty and vacant like an empty cocoon waiting to shelter someone. Tonye remembered the house being so full of life, but now it was so empty and lifeless that one could hear the echoes from one's own breath. Aside from the caretaker and a few other family members living in the big house, the house was unoccupied. Even with the continuous rhythmic tapping sound of the rainfall on the roof, and the whirring from the old ceiling fan up above that was so shaky that Tonye thought it would drop right on top of him, and the loud traditional Ijaw music that streamed out of the caretaker's bedroom, nothing seemed to be entering Tonye's ears. Swathed in deep thoughts, nothing at all seemed to be distracting him. Everywhere was as silent as a graveyard shift in the dead of night at the Ikoyi cemetery.

He thought of Laju, the woman he loved and wanted to spend the rest of his life with and he realized that the butterflies in his stomach no longer fluttered at the mere thought of her. The thought of her no longer sent shivers down his spine and caused his hairs to stand on edge. The thought of her did not send a sudden rush of blood to his brain that caused him to have an instant erection.

He was scared.

That was not a good sign. He thought of the look she had on her face when she had come out to meet him from Grandmother Dawson's house. She bore a sadness on her face that he knew she was trying hard to hide. No matter how much he tried to reach out to her, he knew that her sadness was not something he could take away with a snap of his fingers. He thought of how much he longed for her and how she was moving away from him. Grandmother Dawson's harsh words earlier that day had reminded him for the last time that Laju was not his. No matter how much he professed his love to her and her to him, they were not married yet and the great Dawson matriarch still had a heavy hold on her life. He felt alone, more alone with every passing moment and unsure if a battle with the powerful Dawson matriarch was something he could win.

After the meeting with the matriarch, which ended in nothing short of a disaster, Tonye had gone to drop Laju off at her Auntie's house in the same neighborhood as Grandmother Dawson's. Laju had refused to leave the car until Tonye reassured her that he still loved her, and that what they were going through was a phase which would pass by. As he spoke to her, he wondered if what he was saying was true. He hoped he wasn't wrong. Laju had left him in tears and she had made him promise that he would never leave her, no matter what happened. And he was ready to live up to his words.

Now sitting alone in that old bedroom filled with ancient memories, he wondered if he could hold on long enough to his one true love. His fear was beyond whether he could hold on to Laju, but whether she could hold on to him. For all he knew Grandmother Dawson might already know of some rich, handsome, and eloquent Itsekiri man ready to sweep her off her feet. For all he knew Laju may have already given up on them.

Tonye shook his head to shake off the thoughts that were clouding his head. He rubbed his eyes and heaved a sigh. For the first time since he walked into the house like a zombie, he realized it had stopped raining, and that the last of the setting appeared at the horizon. He stood up and walked to the window. A smile appeared on his face as he saw children running around and jumping in the muddy puddle of rainwater that had gathered in front of the house. He and his younger sister used to run around like that when they were little. And then their mother would come with a whip and send them fleeing for their lives. He shook his head again as the thought of his present predicament overshadowed his childhood memories.

Laju was his life; his everything. Without her, his history was somehow shapeless and incomplete. She made him the gentleman he was, and he could not stand to see her taken away from him like that by some grumpy old-fashioned woman. He *would* not stand for it.

A child playing outside with the other children called out to him and he smiled and waved at the excited little beings. If only the little boy knew that his heart was in a faraway land, lost, finding it hard to find a way back. If only the little soul knew how much he longed to be a child once again and experience freedom.

He pulled the curtains together and walked back to the bed. He sat down. As he sank into the soft foam, he felt like he was falling into an abyss from whence there was no coming back.

"A penny for your thoughts," Laju's familiar voice brought him back to reality.

He jumped. There she was, standing at the doorway like the silhouette of an angel. It was as if a bright shining light shone behind her as she stood there with a warm smile on her face. His heart melted as he rushed to her and took her into his arms.

"Hi baby. Jesus, you scared me. When did you come in? What are you doing here? How did you…" he began as he held her and smelled her hair. She smelled like lavender and roses.

"Easy there, cowboy. One question at a time. And be careful not to break me," she said in a giggle. He released her. "Sorry if I startled you. My auntie's driver said he could find his way here, so I had him bring me. You gave me the address, remember."

"Thank God for him. Gosh you look even more

beautiful than ever."

"Stop it T, you're just saying that." Laju wished Tonye could see the ponies galloping in her stomach.

"But it's true. Plus, I've been thinking about you. About us," he said.

"I have been thinking about you too," she said. She could hear his heartbeat speed up. She looked into his eyes, there were tears welled up inside. Her eyes began to well up too.

"Is something the matter?" She asked.

He shook his head and led her to the bed.

"Nothing's wrong baby. It's just that I do love you, you know that, don't you?" Tonye said wiping away a tear before it got to his cheek.

"I know that, my love. And I love you too. I'm sorry about my grandmother…"

"Shh. Don't say anything. It doesn't matter." He pulled her to him and planted a kiss on her lips. He felt her lips part and he could interpret her longing as she held his head and kissed him like she had never done before.

Tonye pulled away and looked into her deep brown eyes. He saw love. He slipped away from the bed and knelt in front of her.

"Promise me Laju…" he began.

"Anything T, anything."

"Promise me you'll never leave me. Promise that you'll always be here no matter what," he fought back the tears.

"I promise you that with all my heart Tonye. I love you," Laju said as tears rolled down her beautiful almond-shaped face.

"I love you, too," Tonye said.

He kissed her again and then began to lift her blouse and take it over her head. Laju was in total surrender. He stood up and pulled her to her feet. Then he began to kiss her neck.

Laju moaned as Tonye kissed the nape of her neck and with one hand began to undo the hook of her bra. Shivers of pleasure began to crawl on her skin as she longed for more. She unbuttoned his shirt and he let her remove it. She traced her hands on his heavy-set defined muscular chest and made her way down, past his six-pack abs, to his belt buckle. She undid the buckle and unzipped the zipper in what seemed like forever. She didn't want to rush.

Tonye let his trousers fall to the ground.

He cupped one of her breasts as he kissed his way down from her neck to the treasure that was in his hand.

Laju moaned as Tonye's lips encircled her full round breast. She fell back onto the bed and Tonye followed, without letting go for one second.

Both naked, both in fiery passion. Tonye let himself in and Laju held herself from screaming out in utter passion. He was big, and strong, and hot and she wanted him deeper than ever before. She grabbed his back and pulled him even closer as he rocked her on the old creaky bed.

Thunder struck, and lightning flashed, and the two lovers intertwined as one remained unmoved. Cool, misty breeze blew into the room as the rain increased outside but Tonye and Laju had only just begun.

Tonye did not care for the pain on his back as Laju dug her nails into him; he did not care that the creaky bed might soon give in and send them both to the ground in a crash; he did not even care that the rain had blown open the flush windows and was blowing into the room. Nor did he worry that the room wasn't locked, and that anyone could walk in without knocking. All he could think about was the fact that he could not think of anything else but the woman he was one with at that very moment.

Shockwaves travelled all over Laju's body as her strong and hard lover took her to pleasurable heights that she never knew were attainable. She could feel him deep now, deep inside her spring of passion drinking from her fountain of love. She entered another world with him as their sweat glued them to each other. They both trembled like the house shook from a terrible earthquake. She was close. She grabbed on to him and pulled him in even harder.

Tonye and Laju both moaned as they reached their peak. A crackle of thunder, a buzz of lightning and the rain too seemed to have reached its zenith.

Tonye stood up and went over to close the windows. There was a little puddle of water on the floor near the window. He smiled and walked back to the bed.

As he lay down on his back, he cringed a little.

"I'm sorry about your back," Laju said and chuckled.

"It's okay. I'm used to that. It'll heal. Want to take a bath?"

She smiled and nodded.

Three hours later, the rain having subsided, Laju sat down and listened to Tonye speak.

He chose his words with care when he continued.

"Baby, I love you more than anything else in this world and I am ready to make you my wife. But from the way things went with your grandmother, I don't think you are ready to be my wife just yet," Tonye said; his hands were on her laps.

"What do you mean? Of course, I'm ready. Tonye I love you. It is you I want. With time everyone will see that," she began.

"But time is just what we do not have, Laju. We came here to Warri for your grandmother's blessings and so far, so good, I don't see that happening anytime soon."

"But it will. I know it will," Laju began to caress his face but Tonye removed her hands and stood up. He walked to the windows and opened them. He looked outside, the children were gone. He felt his beacon of hope dwindle. From his periphery he could see Laju walking to him. He didn't turn. She stood behind him and slipped her arms around his waist. Her firm breasts pressed on his aching and sore back. He patted her hands but did not turn from the window to face her neither did he say anything.

They both stood there in silence.

Things were not indeed happening as Tonye had hoped. He had hoped that by now they would have set a date for the formal engagement and introduction party and then returned to the UK; but he wasn't seeing that happening so far.

Just then an exquisite black Mercedes Benz drove into the compound and parked right in front of the house. A young man came out from the driver's seat and looked up at him. He didn't say anything; instead, he began to walk to the front porch. Tonye wondered who the young man was. He didn't have any old friends still living in Warri and he doubted if Mr. Agoloma, the caretaker was expecting any visitors of that caliber.

"What are we going to do?" Laju whispered into his back.

Tonye heaved a sigh and continued to examine the exquisite black Mercedes Benz that the mysterious young man had just pulled up in.

"Baby, we'll talk about this some other time. Right now, I just want to figure things out," he said squinting to see if he could make out the young man's face just before he moved away from his view. He must be at the door already because at that instant Tonye heard the doorbell ringing from the hallway.

"But Tonye…"

"Laju," he turned to face her, "We'll talk about it later. Let's not ruin a good moment with the troubles we're facing," he paused and managed a smile before continuing, "We will get through this together. Maybe not today."

Laju was silent as she walked to the bed. Tonye followed her.

"Perhaps I should leave," she said as she picked up her handbag.

Just then there was a gentle knock on the door.

"Just a minute," Tonye called out as he held Laju's shoulders and squeezed, looking into her eyes. "I do love you, and nothing will take that away. I hope you understand that," he said wiping the streak of tear that rolled down her left cheek.

She nodded and sniffed. He held her in an embrace that felt like it would go on forever but the knock on the door came again.

"Let me get this," he said into her ears.

She nodded. It was as if something had taken away her voice.

Tonye opened the door and peered out. It was Mr. Agoloma the caretaker, telling him that he had a visitor.

"Here to see me? Are you sure?" Tonye asked.

"Well, he said he is from Chief Warebi."

"Heavens! Chief Warebi? That's my godfather. Do tell him I'll be with him in a minute," Tonye said and closed the door after the caretaker left.

He smiled. That explained the luxury car and all.

"Baby, can you manage home alone? I have a visitor from Chief Warebi. I've told you about him I guess."

"Yeah, your godfather. Don't worry, I can manage alone," she said managing a smile. He planted a warm kiss on her lips before leading her out of the room.

The young man sprang to his feet as Tonye and Laju walked into the living room.

"Hello. My name is Tonye Kemefa. Could you just give me a minute, let me see that my fiancée here gets a taxi home?" Tonye said offering his hand to the man's already extended hand.

"Please, by all means. Good afternoon madam," he greeted Laju with a nod.

Laju smiled and replied before she left with Tonye.

"You didn't tell the gentleman my name," Laju said as they stood by the road looking out for a taxi.

Tonye turned to look at her, puzzled.

"And it's troubling you because…" He had a smile on his face but that was only to conceal the anger beginning to set in because he already knew where she was driving at.

"Well, I don't know. Perhaps you didn't want him to know that I am Itsekiri," Laju finished and turned to avoid the spark in Tonye's eyes.

Tonye laughed after a short pause.

"But babe, I didn't even get his own name. I didn't intend to do any introductions because I don't even know the young man."

"I'm sorry I brought it up."

"It's alright. But I am not ashamed of you, in case you

are dying to know that. It most hasn't come to that. Heavens! Laju, how can I not be proud of the woman I fell in love with? Do not let the singular incident at your grandmother's house spoil what we've built together."

She was silent.

Tonye took her in his arms just as he saw a taxi. He flagged it down and it came to a halt beside them.

"I love you," he whispered into her ears. She sniffed. He knew she was crying but he didn't say a word to console her, instead he patted her on the back and held her.

"I'll see you soon," she said as she detached herself from his embrace and got into the taxi. She closed the door and stuck her head out if the window and whispered, "I love you too" as the taxi drove away.

*

"I'm sorry to have kept you waiting," Tonye said, re-joining his guest.

The young man sprang up to his feet again as Tonye walked in. Tonye was getting a bit uncomfortable with that.

"So how is Chief Warebi? My caretaker tells me you're from him?" Tonye said, trying to read the man's face. There was nothing written there. He decided to hear what he had to say.

"Chief is fine. He asked me to bring you to his house," the man replied.

Tonye was silent.

"Are you serious? Like, now?"

"Yes sir. Right away."

"Well then, I'd better go change into something else," Tonye said and began to leave for his bedroom. He knew it would be pointless to probe the young man about what the Chief wanted to see him about. Or how he even got to know he was in town when he's been keeping a low profile ever since he and Laju got into Warri.

A few moments later the young man opened the right side of the back-passenger's seat for Tonye, but the latter smiled and declined.

"I think I'll ride shotgun," Tonye said.

"Pardon me?" The man had a puzzled look on his face. He hadn't come across that expression before.

Tonye smiled.

"I'm sorry. I said I'd rather ride with you in front."

As the car set in motion, Tonye wondered why the Chief had sent a driver to come fetch him in that fashion. It was true that he had not seen him in a while, especially since his return from England, but he had a sick feeling that something was not right. He had enough to deal with now and he just hoped that his godfather was just excited about his return and nothing else. The old man could be dramatic sometimes. Tonye thought.

The rest of the drive to Chief Warebi's estate passed in silence and Tonye didn't mind. At least it gave him some time to think, and as usual the Ijaw music streaming from the car stereo did nothing to jaunt him out of yet another thinking spree.

Six.

Mogha and Seye

MY DEAR BOYS, *I wish that you are not reading this letter right now, but if you are, that means you have fallen into a trap from which I have just escaped. I have just spoken with your sister and she told me that you two had planned to surprise me with your return home. That would have been a pleasant surprise but given the present circumstances; I wish you two were as far away from this city as you could be.*

My bosom friend, Uncle Preye called me only a few hours ago and gave me news that was heart-breaking. He told me that he had gathered from sources that I have become a target for elimination by the growing Ijaw militants who think that I am a threat to them and their movement to reclaim Warri from the hands of the Itsekiris. I do not know how they produced that ridiculous idea. In truth, I don't want to know. All I am concerned about right now is your safety. If you have come home and are reading this letter, then you must leave at once. There is enough money in the case I left behind, for the both of you. I want you to take the money and leave. I have gone to Benin City to your Uncle's house. I will be there for a week, waiting for you. Charter a taxi if you must and get to Benin City as soon as possible. I don't know what to do right now.

I don't know if fleeing for my life without making sure whether you were safe was terrible. For that, I am sorry. I love you two with all my life and I will do anything to make sure you are alright. Please, my sons, tarry no further and leave.

With all my love,

Your father, Jonah.

The silence in the room was so thick that one could slice right through it. The boys' gaze stuck to the piece of paper they both held. Their hands were trembling. It was as if the paper had become too heavy for just one person to hold. They could not hear the rain outside anymore, so it was obvious that it had stopped.

Seye let go of the letter and turned to look at his brother. His eyes filled with tears that refused to drop. If only Mogha could hear the pounding in his heart. If only his brother could see how scared he was, and how much he needed him to be strong for them both. He opened his mouth to speak but nothing came out. His throat was dry, and he had lost his voice. He cleared his throat and tried again.

"W--What are we going to do now?" Seye managed to say as his older brother stood up and began to pace.

Mogha turned to look at his brother.

"You heard what Daddy said, we have to get out of here now. So, come on, let's get our things and leave. It's stopped raining already," Mogha said and held out his hand to his brother.

Just then a heavy knock came from the door. The two

boys froze and listened. The sound came again. This time they heard keys jangling against each other. Someone was trying to use a key to get in.

Mogha turned to his brother as he placed a finger on his lips. He walked to their father's wardrobe and began to rummage through it. He seemed to have become swallowed by the wardrobe before he pulled out a bag.

"What's that?" Seye whispered.

"Shh. I've seen Daddy keep them here once," Mogha said still not making sense.

"What are you talking about? Keep 'what' there?" Seye insisted.

"I said keep it down. Guns. I've seen Daddy keep his guns here before, in this bag," Mogha said as he used something to destroy the small padlock that fastened the two zippers together.

"Gun! I never knew Daddy had guns," Seye went on.

"Well, now you know and guess what, you're about to get the quickest lesson on how to use one too."

Seye was silent as Mogha opened the bag to reveal two modern hunting rifles and with packets of bullets. Seye's eyes widened as he watched his brother handle the weapons with dexterity. It was as if Mogha had handled a gun before. Or had he? But Seye did not ask any questions.

The sound came again. This time the door was shutting close. Someone had let himself him.

"*They* are inside. Here, hold this," Mogha said in fast,

short sentences as he held out the now loaded weapon to his brother.

Seye grabbed the gun and examined it, whilst he wondered why his brother spoke so fast, but he didn't say anything.

Mogha heaved a heavy sigh and turned to his brother.

"Seye, no matter what happens today, I want you to be strong and know that I love you. Now just follow my lead," Mogha said and held up the gun in a shooting stance. Hot sweat rolled down his forehead.

Sounds of movement came from downstairs again.

Mogha stood up and motioned to his brother to remain in the room and be alert while he went to check out who had broken in. Seye began to protest but Mogha hushed him and turned to leave.

Mogha did not consider himself to be a brave young man. But given the drama that had been unfolding before them in the past few hours since they arrived home, every passing second seemed to be defining his every move. He wondered what his younger brother would be going through, and he just wished he would get them away from there.

As he made his way downstairs with the butt plate of the rifle tugged at his right shoulder and his finger on the trigger, Mogha wondered if he had it in him to pull the trigger. His heartbeat increased by a double and the tugging headache made him feel like his head would explode.

He got to the foot of the stairs without incidence and

walked into the sitting room. His heart jumped out of his mouth when the intruder turned to face him.

"Jesus Christ!" Uncle Preye said throwing his hands up in the air in total surrender.

"Oh my God! Uncle Preye!" Mogha screamed as he lowered the weapon and rushed to hug the man, he'd known all his life as Uncle Preye. His father's best friend and trusted business ally.

"Jesus! Boy, where did you get a gun?" The man asked, holding his chest.

"Uncle Preye, I'm sorry. I thought you were someone else," Mogha said instead avoiding his Uncle Preye's question.

"When did you boys come in?" The middle-age man asked, still trying to recover from the shock.

"About an hour ago. Uncle what's going on?" Mogha asked.

"I don't know. Where is your brother?"

"He's upstairs."

"There's no time to explain. You must leave now. My car is parked outside; I'll drive you to where you can catch a taxi out of town," Uncle Preye said heading for the stairs.

"My father said he would be waiting for us in Benin City."

"Benin City? When did you speak with him?" Uncle Preye asked and turned to look at the young man still holding the rifle.

"Well, he dropped us a letter before he left in case we came while he was gone. And a briefcase full of dollars saying we might need the money," Mogha said trailing behind his uncle.

Uncle Preye laughed and shook his head as he continued making his way upstairs.

"Jonah. Typical of him," he muttered under his breath.

Seye jumped to his feet as he saw Uncle Preye.

"How are you my boy?" Uncle Preye asked hugging the younger of the brothers who was about a foot taller than him.

"I'm fine sir. Uncle we need to get out of here," Seye reiterated.

"Yes, we do. I came over to lock up and pick up any valuable document your father might have left behind. I didn't think you'd be here. I'm glad to see you two but now we must leave. Terrible things have been happening around the city and it is not safe for anyone right now."

"Uncle, what's going on?" Mogha asked again.

"It seems that war has broken out between Ijaw and Itsekiri youths. A few hours ago, an Itsekiri militia set a small Ijaw village on fire and the Ijaw retaliation around town has been terrible. I can't even begin to go into the cause of these stupid violent uprising. Can't we just settle our differences in a more civilized manner?" he asked himself than anyone.

The boys were silent as Uncle Preye muttered to himself.

Seye broke away from the others and began to walk towards the window. Then he stopped on his tracks. He began to shake. Unable to speak, he turned to Mogha and beckoned on him with a wave of his hands – he'd earlier dropped the other rifle on the bed. Mogha walked to him and he too froze to the ground at what he saw outside their house.

Uncle Preye walked up to them. He froze too.

A few yards away, a group of men was walking towards the house. Uncle Preye, Mogha and Seye did not need God to tell them who they were and what they were coming for. The machetes in their hands, the guns they held, the gallons they carried, the looks on their faces; the boys knew that the war had come to their door step.

"Oh my God!" Uncle Preye did not know what else to say.

The boys looked onto the middle-aged man for their next move.

"Just stay here, I'll go outside and tell them no one is in here. They'll believe me since there are no cars outside. Do not make a move. And boys, hold on to those guns, they may come in handy," the man said as he began to rush out of the room.

"Seye, grab the other gun and stay behind the bed. I'll be here beside the window and be on the lookout. I'm sure they won't see me from here," Mogha said in a quick sentence.

Seye nodded and went for his gun. He readied himself the way he'd seen Mogha do earlier and waited.

That was it. If only they'd waited a little longer in Lagos they wouldn't be in that situation, Seye found himself thinking. He shook his head and tried to focus but he couldn't. He'd been trying so hard to be as strong as his brother, but he knew he wasn't. He knew he was not as strong as Mogha. Mogha was born a leader; he knew just what to do at the right time. He knew how to handle about any situation. Given the way he'd been handling things so far, one would think that he was in the military or something. Seye took a quick glance at the rifle that was in his hand and he increased his grip on it. He was ready for whatever would come through their front door. He looked over at Mogha crouched down beside the window and he admired his brother. He wished he was as strong as him.

Uncle Preye was just locking the doors outside when the mob got to the house. He turned to face them with a smile on his face.

He began to speak to them in the Ijaw dialect to show some form of brotherliness.

"What are you doing here?" one who seemed like the head of the mob asked looking at Preye, who had started to walk towards them to meet them half-way at the entrance of the compound before they get in.

"Oh. Nothing much. The former occupant is my friend. He dropped his keys for me before he left. I was just making a round that's all," Preye said. A little panic leaked from his shaky voice.

"Is that so? So, there's no one in there?" the leader asked.

"Yes. I mean no one," Preye replied.

"People like you are the ones selling us out to the Itsekiris," someone from within the crowd shouted and threw a stone at Preye.

Preye took a step backward.

"Yes. Na una dey make friends with Itsekiri people," another one shouted in support of his comrade who'd made the first comment.

"It's not like that. We've been friends since childhood," Preye said, trying to make sense.

"Does it matter? It's the same thing," the leader said and stepped up to Preye. He peered into his eyes. His bloodshot eyes examined the trembling man's.

"Are you telling me the truth that there's no one in this house?" he asked again.

"Y—yes. There's no one around. He skipped town earlier today."

"By 'he' I'm sure you mean Engineer Aroromi. He is one of those people who use the money they get from our oil to bribe the government to change the Warri South-West local government to Ogidigben. You think we don't know?" the leader said.

Preye shook his head in disagreement but didn't utter a word.

"Surprised? We know who our enemies are Mr. Preye. We are not fighting an empty war as people like you seem to think."

Preye stood rooted to the ground unable to move. He

wished there was some way to escape his present predicament, but he wasn't going to leave unless the mob left first.

"Raze the house," the mob leader said. Preye's heart froze.

"Please my brother," Preye began in Ijaw and before he could say any further, a heavy blow landed on his face.

"Who is your brother, you traitor? Don't call me 'brother'," the leader shouted as Preye cowered holding his hurting face. Hot tears gathered in his eyes. No, he wasn't crying, the blow dealt to him was so strong that it stung his eyes.

The mob began to advance towards the house and pour fuel around the compound. Grenades made with empty bottles filled with fuel and a trailing wick from its mouth, were at the ready.

Preye fell to his knees and began to plead.

"Please, don't burn the house. Let peace reign," he didn't know what he was saying, if he did, he wouldn't have said it because, yet another blow was dealt to him. This time it was from the butt of a gun.

"Raze the house to the ground," the leader of the mob shouted again.

Preye looked around for help. There was no one in sight. It's funny how people vanish in the face of danger. Not that he blamed them. The entire street was empty. There was little movement. Preye looked up and for the first time noticed the smoke rising hope to the heavens on the horizon. A few yards away from his left, a house was already ablaze. An Itsekiri man's house, nonetheless. He looked up to the sky and prayed for rain, but the rain had come and gone when no one needed it. He thought of his best-friend's children trapped inside their own house that was about to send smoke sacrifices up to the gods. He wished there was something he could do to help them now. He couldn't risk opening to the leader of the mob that there were two young boys trapped within the house and that they should spare them. God knew what the outcome of that would be.

By now the mob had begun to set fire to the house and the fire gained ground.

Preye closed his eyes and began to weep.

"Hey, I saw someone just now in the house. I swear I saw someone. There's someone in this house!" one of the mobsters shouted, pointing up to a window at the upper deck of the house.

The leader walked up to Preye and looked down at him with all the anger in the world reflecting in his eyes.

"I thought you said there was no one in the house," the man asked, bringing out his sidearm tucked in his trouser.

Preye looked up at him in tears, "They are children for God's sake. They are just children," he said.

The shot was clean and sudden. Even Preye could not have expected it. He must have died within seconds of the shot because the bullet caught him right in-between his eyes. He slumped backwards.

Moments after Preye died, there was a responding gunshot from the house and the leader of the mod lay dead too beside his earlier victim. It all happened so fast and it was like a scene from a Hollywood movie. Pandemonium broke loose and the entire mob rushed at the house as if the house itself caused the death of their comrade leader. But they were soon faced with three major challenges: first, they had set the perimeter on fire and the fire was fast spreading, so they risked getting hurt themselves if they went any closer to the house; second, the door was impossible to break in through; third, the windows were made with thick bulletproof glass. So, even as they set their guns blazing and opened fire at the house, it wasn't of much use.

They decided on avenging the death of their fallen leader, so they set to work to try to break into the fortitude that was Aroromi's mansion.

Moments earlier

Mogha spied from the window as Uncle Preye began to speak with the leader of the mob. He could tell from the way the man spoke, that he was the leader. He adjusted his position, to not make any detectable movement while he placed the long nuzzle of the gun on the window pane. He looked through the scope of the gun, but it was blurry. He adjusted it until he could make out the images.

"What do you see?" Seye asked in a whisper but loud enough for Mogha to hear him.

"Shh. A group of guys with guns and gallons of

petrol."

"Fuel? How could you be so sure?"

"Because the Kayodes' house three blocks away is on fire. And oh, houses are on fire everywhere around us. How come we didn't notice that when we came in?" Mogha asked the last part to himself.

"Beats me. What do you see now?"

"Uncle Preye is talking to them. Jesus Christ!" Mogha exclaimed and placed his free hand over his mouth.

"What happened, what happened?" Seye asked. He was getting anxious.

"One of them just hit Uncle Preye on the face. I mean, the blow threw him to the ground."

"I'm coming over there," Seye said and began to move.

"Seye, stay where you are. What do you think you are doing? Do you want to get us both killed?" Mogha asked and Seye stopped.

Mogha's eyes widened and he withdrew the gun and looked over at his brother. Seye could tell something was happening that Mogha wasn't saying.

"You'd better tell me what's going on there right now or else I'll come over," He threatened.

"They've started to burn *our* house."

"What? *Burn* our house?"

The boys were silent. Seye sprang to his feet and began to rush towards Mogha at the window. Before Mogha could protest, Seye was already crouching beside him. Mogha sensed someone would detect them, so it didn't come as a shock to him when he began to hear someone shout amidst the mob that there was someone in the house.

"Seye, they now know we're in here. Happy now?" Mogha whispered.

Seye mouthed the words *I'm sorry* but Mogha ignored him.

Then there was a gunshot.

The boys' hearts stopped beating for a few seconds. Mogha resumed his former firing position and looked through the scope of the gun. His heart melted away. His head exploded. His bladder went off. His eyes widened.

There, filling the vision of the rifle scope lay dead on the floor his beloved Uncle Preye. A man they'd come to know as a part of their family. A man who was his godfather.

Mogha didn't think. He didn't even hear Seye ask him about what had happened, he just reacted. He zeroed his vision on the head of the man who had just shot his godfather and just squeezed the trigger. His finger had been on the trigger guard since, so squeezing it was not hard for him. He didn't think much of the pain that shot through his shoulder after he pressed the trigger; that much he could bear. It was the pain of losing someone so dear to him that he could not bear. It was the pain of seeing humans act like animals that he could not bear. The pain had just made him a murderer and that too, he could not bear. He began to weep and wet himself at the same time. He'd lost control of his urinary organ.

The mob responded to Mogha's assault as they opened fire on the house. Bullets whizzed past the open window into the room as the brothers crouched by the corner of the wall where they were quite out of reach, at least for the moment. After what seemed like a split second, the gunshots reduced and everywhere was dead calm. But the war was far from over and the boys knew it.

"They killed him! They fucking killed Uncle Preye. And now I just killed a man," Mogha wept, burying his head in his younger brother's chest. Seye wept as he made sense of what had just occurred. He held his brother and patted his back. Mogha's body trembled with heavy sobs.

Then the noise resumed; heavy poundings on the door. The boys had one explanation for that: the mob was trying to break in.

"Seye are you alright?" Mogha asked, looking at his brother.

"I'm fine. Why are you looking at me like that?" Seye asked.

"I---I think you are bleeding," Mogha replied. "I---I think you have been shot."

Seven.

Toritseju and Jolomi

DOCTOR TORITSEJU BENSON could not concentrate on work in the hospital. The events of the past few days had left her weak and without a will to go on. Every day now there was a new burnt victim and all the stories were the same, although a few had some twisted and horrific variety to them. Some said they were asleep in their homes when the fire started. Others said they were walking on their own minding their own business. And for what? For being in the wrong place at the wrong time? Or belonging to the *wrong* ethnic group. Who would do such things to fellow human beings? Now she spent more time in the operation theater trying to help some of these people. Some of them suffered such severe burns that they would have to live with the scars for the rest of their lives. She wasn't a plastic surgeon and even an attempt at a reconstructive procedure may not have led anywhere.

For once, she wished she had attended those free cosmetic surgery lectures Dr. Zipora had offered to them while she was still in medical school in New York. She could not handle a plastic surgeon, she'd told her friends. She wanted to be able to help *real* people with *real* medical conditions. So, while her friends jumped at the opportunity to rub shoulders with the elite plastic surgeons that Dr. Zipora was bringing with him to his lectures, daring his students to dream of having a chance to practice in Los Angeles or Miami or Hollywood doing boob-jobs, facelifts and Botox for the stars, she stuck with general practice and dreamt of joining Doctor Beyond Borders. Even now she wondered if most of her classmates realized their dreams.

Toju walked to her office window at the General Hospital in Warri and looked outside. Just a few days ago no one knew what was coming. Now the city looked more deserted with every passing minute. People had begun to leave, family after family. The trail of smoke still made its way upward into the sky. She let her eyes take her on a panoramic journey across where it could see and there was nothing much left to see. A once vibrant city now lay dead. The silence was so intense that one could hear the wailing of a child who had just lost her mother, from a distance.

Toju closed her eyes tight and tears escaped down her beautiful face.

It was official, Warri was under siege and there was no one coming to their rescue.

Thoughts of Jolomi overshadowed her mind. Where could he be today? He had left early that morning before dawn to attend a covert meeting with Chief Warebi. She prayed for his safety. A gathering of a bunch of Ijaw and Itsekiri people pursuing a common cause would make them easy target. She was so proud of him and what he was doing to help stop the war, but she wanted him safe. That was all she wanted.

She thought of how she had first met Jolomi two years ago in Bellevue Medical Center at the New York University. How, two years ago, she almost lost him in Rwanda. She let a smile linger on her face as she allowed her mind to take a journey to the past. That day when a man lost his heart and gained a new one.

*

Toju's beeper began to beep. It jolted her from what seemed to have been a ten-second nap. She picked up the little device from a small stool on the corner of the bed in the small room resident doctors went to, to steal a few moments of rest and she felt like flinging it at the wall. She sighed when she saw on the display that it was the Chief Resident asking her to come back. She grabbed her stethoscope hanging from a hook on the wall and wrapped it around her neck as she made for the door. She looked at her wristwatch; it was a quarter to eight in the night. She shook her head. What could the Chief Resident want now? She was supposed to be on a time out. All her friends were moonlighting somewhere and making some extra cash, but there she was, stuck with making rounds.

"Doctor Toju, I was just on my way to get you. CR wants you," a nurse said, running into her.

"Yeah I know. She already beeped me like a million times," Toju said as she walked on, the nurse joining her.

"She wants you in the ER."

"The ER? I thought there's supposed to be a heart transplant going on there right now."

"Yes, there is. She wants to see you up at the observatory," the nurse said.

Toju stopped.

"Angela, what's going on?" Toju asked when the nurse also stopped and turned to face her.

"I don't know doctor. But I'm sure it's nothing serious."

"I sure hope so too."

The nurse returned to her station as Toju entered the empty observation room and began to watch the team of doctors perform the heart transplant scheduled there. Toju still could not guess why the Chief Resident wanted her there. Now she was more worried about her lack of sleep and the fact that she was on-call that night than anything else for that matter. The door of the observation room swung open and the Chief Resident, a petite Caucasian woman in her early forties walked in. From the way she looked and spoke, it was obvious she had vast medical experience.

"Toju I'm sorry for calling you out like this. I'm sure you must have escaped to fantasy Island when I beeped," she teased as she went to stand beside her.

"It's no biggie. So, what's up Doc? Did I forget to submit my chart or what?" Toju asked.

"Not that. The patient in there, we need your help with him."

"Okay. So, what can I do? The room is already sterilized and sealed off, I can't go in,"

the Chief Resident laughed.

"You're such a funny girl. The doctors are doing fine. The patient, he's a Nigerian and he has some similar unpronounceable words in his medical file as you do on your employment forms. We need you to take care of him for a while when he goes in to the ICU."

Toju was silent for a while.

"Wait a minute Doc. You want *me* to babysit a full-grown man just because he's Nigerian?"

"Actually, yes," the woman snapped back.

It was not the first time a Nigerian received treatment in the hospital and she had never babysat any Nigerian patients before. Why this one?

"Doc, I'm sorry but why?" Toju asked.

"I feel it's the right thing to do. If he wakes up it'll be nice to see a pretty face," the doctor teased, laughed and left.

Toju remained frozen to the spot before she grabbed a chair and sat down. It was a funny situation. Because *he had some similar unpronounceable words in his medical file as you do on your employment forms.* What kind of an excuse was that? She couldn't help but wonder. She thought they were asking her to stay away from her usual routine because one of her patients had died the day before. But patients die every day from complications that are not the fault of the doctors. Even the CR told her, she had done all she could do to save the little girl. Toju crossed her hands over her breast and sulked.

She noticed in the operating room that the surgery was over. The anaesthesiologist was administering a doze to the patient and the doctors began to leave. Toju's eyes went to the ECG, and she watched his heart rate for a while. The heart seemed to be doing fine. Toju peered at the patient's face but she could not make out anything except for the fact that he was black.

Moments later after the surgery, specialized nurses came in to wheel the patient off to recovery at the ICU. Toju stood up and left the OR. She was getting herself ready for her new assignment.

"Um, excuse me, Dr. Richards," Toju called after one of the doctors. She noticed he was following the nurses. He held a file and Toju guessed it belonged to the patient.

"Ah. If it isn't the young and beautiful Dr. Toju. What brings you to our surgical suites? Tired of the hustle and bustle of the ER, are we?" the handsome Canadian doctor said as Toju joined him on the walk to the elevators.

"Of course, not doctor. How's your patient doing?" she asked leaning over to steal a look at the file. Richards snapped it close and turned to her with a warm smile. He looked somewhere around thirty-eight and forty but very good-looking for his age.

"*Our* patient you mean."

"Emmm…" Toju stammered.

"Dr. Tracy already told me she'd be sending you

down. Let me guess, you've agreed that you have a thing for us surgeons, huh," he teased.

"You're funny Richards. But, am I needed?" Toju asked and Richards stopped to look at her.

"Toju my guess is Dr. Tracy is still impressed with your surgical performances while you were still a medical intern and somehow hopes she could turn you over to join us. That's just a guess. I'd say she feels you do a rather excellent job taking care of patients."

"Yeah right. I'm not a nurse, Richards, I'm a medical doctor."

"Uh! Feisty. I never said you were a nurse, *Doctor* Toju. Just saying you are a pretty darn great doctor. That's all," Richard concluded with a serious look on his face.

"Oh! Thank you."

"Hey, don't get ahead of yourself. It's not something you haven't heard about a million times already," Richards said and they both laughed.

"I told her I didn't want to be with you guys. I love being in the ER."

"Well, what do you know? You are here now, aren't you? Here, this is his file, go through it. I'm sure you'll make out a thing or two. You're a smart kid," he said handing over the file to her.

"Thank you for your vote of confidence, doctor."

"You are most welcome. Well, this is where I get off. I have no business in the ICU. At least not right now," he said with a warm smile. Toju wondered what his story was and why he was still single.

"You are such a devil, Richards."

"A handsome one no less," he chuckled and Toju's heart missed a beat.

"Oh, I better get a move on then. See you around doc."

"You too," he said and turned to leave.

As Toju rode down to the ICU, she opened the file and went through it. There was nothing *unpronounceable* about what she read; even his names were simple to get out. Jolomi Benson. Okay, the first name may have been a hard one to crack, but *Benson?* Who couldn't pronounce *Benson?* She smiled at her Chief Resident's sense of humour. This must be one of her ploys to get her to join the team of surgeons who now was lacking a female doctor, that not counting the female anaesthesiologist.

She had another glance at his name.

"Jolomi Benson. Hmm…what's your story hey?" she muttered to herself.

It happened fast. All it took was eight weeks pulled out of a fairy tale. Toju and Jolomi had fallen in love with each other by the time Jolomi was ready to return to his job with the BBC back in London. He had proposed to her and she had said yes without thinking twice about it. Toju didn't care about the risks she was taking, marrying a man who would have to be in London while she remained in New York, all she wanted was to marry the man of her dreams. She had suggested leaving her job and moving in with him, but he had declined, saying he was a field journalist with just one job left and then they would be together in New York again. But all she wanted was to be with him, so as soon as the wedding was over two weeks after his discharge from the hospital, Toju joined the *Doctors Beyond Borders* program and asked to go anywhere they needed doctors, so she could follow Jolomi to all his missions. But that dream never came true. Jolomi went to Rwanda and almost died after he, his assistant and local guide got ambushed on their third day there. They beheaded his assistant, who was a Rwandan national, but a British citizen, shot his tour guide in the head, and Jolomi was to be chopped into pieces, had the United Nations forces not come to his rescue. Jolomi never did come back himself but she was glad he came back, to her. So, the first chance she got after she nursed Jolomi to recovery for the second time, she resigned from her job in New York and decided it was time she returned home to Nigeria with her traumatized husband.

"Doctor, we have another one," her nurse said jolting Toju from her thoughts.

Without saying anything, Toju stood and got to work.

*

The driver, who didn't speak a word to Jolomi since he picked him up that morning, drove to a stop in front of a huge gate and waited for the security to open it. A young man appeared from the compound through a smaller side-gate attached to the big one and walked up to the car. The driver rolled down his window and spoke to the guard in their Ijaw dialect. Jolomi didn't feel too comfortable about that, but he didn't say anything. Soon after, the gates opened, and the black Mercedes Benz drove in.

The car came to a stop in front of a huge mansion and Jolomi moved out.

"This way, sir," the driver said, gesturing for him to follow him.

Jolomi followed in silence as the man took him through the side of the house to another but smaller mansion built just behind the one in front. Jolomi wondered why the Chief had chosen that location for their meeting. The last time he met with Chief Warebi was at the latter's house in town in Warri, and they made him feel welcomed and comfortable. Today, however, not so much. Everything seemed quite different. Was it because he had just spent about four hours on a drive down there with a driver who didn't speak to him? Or, perhaps it was because he had no idea where in the world he was. He doubted if they were still in Delta State because, the road they took which veered off the usual routes he was familiar with didn't look so familiar at all.

Jolomi began to pick up voices as the driver opened the door of the house out back and ushered him in. Jolomi followed like a sheep following someone to slaughter. The funny thing was that he didn't feel the need to do anything about it. As much as he was not comfortable with the drive down there, the moment he heard Chief Warebi's voice, his heart felt comforted.

"Ah, Jolomi, it's nice to see you again. Hope the journey wasn't so stressful," Chief Warebi asked as Jolomi was led into the sitting room. The Chief seemed to be meeting with three other men.

"Good morning sir. Good morning all," Jolomi greeted and was offered a seat.

"I'm sorry for bringing you all the way out here. I saw the need to change the usual venue of our meeting from my home in Warri to this more serene and safer environment," Chief Warebi explained.

"It's alright sir."

"Let me get on with the introductions then. This is Ebidowei Angbare. He is a columnist with *The Eagle* newspaper, and he's been working with me for a long time now. And here is Ayomide Ajamimogha. He is a seasoned political analyst and a regular African political correspondent for *Time* magazine. And this here is my godson," The Chief said, patting the shoulder of a young man sitting next to him. "His name is Tonye Kemefa, he is a lawyer. He has degrees in law and International Diplomatic Relations from universities in London. He will be our legal counsel," the Chief concluded with a smile.

"It's a great honour to meet you all," Jolomi said shaking hands with each of the men.

"Well, everyone, this is Jolomi Benson; international journalist and recipient of a CNN/UN International Journalist Award. That's that, we'll get down to business while we have breakfast."

While they ate breakfast, the Chief explained to the group the gravity of the situation at hand. Itsekiri youths had infiltrated certain Ijaw villages around the coast of Warri and set them on fire whilst looting and other atrocious acts took place. The same thing had been happening with the Ijaw boys going to Itsekiri villages. The war was finding its way into the city. Reports confirmed that Ijaw and Itsekiri boys have set fire to houses in town, belonging to wealthy and influential Itsekiri and Ijaw indigenes.

"I don't know for how long we can take this," the chief said and paused.

He went on to explain that according to his sources, rich men from both warring parties are funding the purchase of the arms used by the growing militia.

"I have had meetings with the Itsekiri chieftains and they assured me that they had no knowledge of anyone supporting or funding the Itsekiri movement against the Ijaws. Our job here is to bring peace to this State and nothing else."

He spoke of a meeting with the Military Governor who said that if the crisis escalated, the Federal Government would declare a state of emergency on Warri.

Jolomi and the other men listened and spoke little while Chief Warebi spoke. The young journalist could feel the passion in the old man's voice. Here was a man who believed in the right cause and was doing everything in his power to achieve it. He glanced around the table and imagined the great deal of trouble the Chief must have gone through to bring all these men together.

After the meeting, the other two men departed leaving Tonye and Jolomi alone with Chief Warebi.

"You two catch up. I need to take a short nap. Hope

you don't mind," Chief Warebi said standing.

"Oh, not at all sir," Jolomi said and both men stood up in courtesy as the Chief stood up to retire into his bedroom.

"Tonye, why don't you tell Jolomi about this beautiful Itsekiri girl you want to marry?" Chief Warebi said with a warm smile.

Tonye smiled back and nodded.

Jolomi could see worry on the young man's face and he didn't need to hear the entire story to know what he might be going through.

Chief Warebi retired and left Tonye and Jolomi alone. It was just the two of them and a bottle of German Brandy.

"So, let me guess, the girl's family is giving you wahala?" Jolomi said. Tonye smiled and nodded. He heaved a dejected sigh and began to speak while Jolomi listened.

Eight.

Oyinmiebi

OYINMIEBI'S HEART wouldn't stop pounding and he feared it would jump out of his mouth if he didn't do something about it. He held his chest as if it would help but his heartbeat increased. It was as if his heart sat trapped within his chest, trying to break free. He stole a glance at his cousin Zuokumo and Zuokumo's very gait was enough to tell him that he didn't have a problem with his own heart trying to flee from his chest cavity.

"Zuokumo, please slow down. You are walking too fast. See, I'm panting," Oyinmiebi said trying to catch his breath as he ran after his cousin.

"Slow down? Wetin dey worry you sef? The meeting was supposed to start like an hour ago but no, I sidon house dey wait for my cousin wen wan begin make-up like a girl before leaving the house," Zuokumo snapped back increasing his pace rather than slowing down.

"Come on bro. I told you I needed to use the toilet," Oyinmiebi tried to defend himself. He wished his cousin believed him and didn't see right through him to know that he was having a typical case of 'cold feet.'

"Abeg e done do. All I want is to get to the meeting on time. Abi I no tell you about am since two days ago? And you have had that much time to think about it, abeg stop to dey complain and waka quick."

Oyinmiebi held his peace and tried as much as possible to keep his thoughts to himself as he ran after his cousin to meet up with his fast-paced walking.

Zuokumo was right. Oyinmiebi had been developing some cold-feet since his last discussion with his cousin about what 'needed to be done' concerning the Itsekiris' oppression over the Ijaws in Warri. And as much as he wanted to be a part of such a revolution, he didn't quite see the point to it. His heart had filled with worries and doubts since then. Zuokumo was not as exposed and educated as he was so he wouldn't look at things from his point of view. All he could see was oppression. He must want to do something about it, but Oyinmiebi did not have a good feeling about going with him to the meeting. What scared him the most was that he had no control over himself. He found himself following Zuokumo, even though he didn't want to go.

Oyinmiebi didn't need anyone to tell him that they had reached the meeting venue. The crowd in front of the huge gate leading into the wide and luxurious compound of Chief Oweila was overwhelming. And the funniest thing about the crowd was that it was getting larger by the minute and more than half of the population consisted of old men, children and even women. Oyinmiebi couldn't help but wonder what Zuokumo meant when he said, 'a meeting of able-bodied men.' The crowd before him had no able-bodied men. Oyinmiebi became worried; no wonder the chief didn't open his gate for 'the whole of Warri' to troop in.

"Zuo I thought you said it was going to be a small meeting. It seems the whole town is here," Oyinmiebi complained.

"Hmm.... you worry too much. Everyone is excited about what's going on. I'm sure they are here to show their support. What is important is that we are doing something about our situation," Zuokumo said, stretching to see ahead of the crowd, ignoring the worried look on Oyinmiebi's face.

Not long after their arrival, Chief Oweila mounted the make-shift stage ahead of the crowd to address them. The shouts and screams of the crowd when he appeared from his compound were ear-piercing. Oyinmiebi still didn't see what the fuss was all about. A man was about to instigate people to start a war and they were happy about it. He wondered how the idea had excited him at all in the first place.

Oyinmiebi could not hear what Chief Oweila was saying. He was too far away for anyone to hear him, and he spoke without the aid of a public address system. Not to mention the fact that those who could hear him screamed and shouted after every word he said. Oyinmiebi looked beside him and Zuokumo had disappeared from his side. No doubt he must have pushed his way into the crowd to try to get closer to his role-model, Chief Oweila. Oyinmiebi sighed, turned, and started heading away from the growing crowd. As he walked towards a shop just close by to buy some water to drink, he saw a far black smoke rise to the sky.

It had already begun. He thought, and the thought scared him to death. He was wise enough to know that wars caused more harm than good.

What was it that the Ijaws and Itsekiris could not work out in civility? He wondered how the change of a local government headquarters from one Ijaw town to an Itsekiri town could cause such commotion.

He bought a bottle of icy water and drank, even as the crowd's screams drowned him deep within it.

*

After the meeting which lasted for five hours, during which Oyinmiebi sat out in the shop drinking one bottle of water after another, he and Zuokumo strolled back home. Zuokumo was back to his chatty self and was filling Oyinmiebi in on what he 'missed' during the meeting. Oyinmiebi walked beside him in silence, buried in his own thoughts and confusions.

Zuokumo spoke of a revolution. He spoke of 'taking back what was theirs.' As Oyinmiebi listened, he knew that Zuokumo was giving him the exact speech of Chief Oweila. He didn't realize how much Zuokumo admired Chief Oweila until then, watching him speak about the man with such vigor and passion. It reminded him of how people talked of Dr. Martin Luther King and it scared him to death because he was not buying what Chief Oweila was selling.

Zuokumo spoke of vengeance. He spoke of retaliation as if he knew for sure who his enemy was. As if he knew for sure whose door to knock on and take vengeance for the crime committed against him.

Zuokumo spoke of war. War! Oyinmiebi was scared. He had always wanted adrenaline pumping through his veins but now, he had bitten off more than what he could chew, and the war was in the works.

"Wait a minute Zuokumo," Oyinmiebi cut his cousin short in mid-sentence. The look on Zuokumo's face was that of anger mixed with irritation but Oyinmiebi did not care.

"What is it?" Zuokumo snapped.

"You speak of such things, but these things are all violence. Can't things happen without the use of violence? Can't there be compromise. Can't...."

"Oh, shut up Oyinmiebi," Zuokumo snapped again.

Oyinmiebi swallowed the rest of his words.

"What do you think you are talking about? You, who have been away in Benin City just around the corner don't seem to know what is going on and those in America and London already know what the Itsekiris are doing to the Ijaws and Urhobos in this Warri. Please, if you don't have anything reasonable to say, don't talk at all."

"I was only trying to..."

"Don't try to do anything. I didn't ask you to go with me today. You alone, made that decision by yourself and now you want to be a saint," Zuokumo said, angry.

"Hey, take it easy on me please. What's wrong with trying to be reasonable?" Oyinmiebi snapped back.

Zuokumo didn't speak further, he knew Oyinmiebi was indeed upset and didn't want to say more so he wouldn't insult him.

The rest of the walk home passed in silence and Oyinmiebi couldn't be more thankful for it. At least he could sit alone in peace with his thoughts. He knew Zuokumo was also deep in thought because he had a certain blank look on his face. When they got to Zuokumo's parents house, Oyinmiebi stayed a while and had dinner with them before heading home. Zuokumo walked him to the main road from where he would get a taxi home and during the walk, they made some petty talk, but no one mentioned the meeting at Chief Oweila's house.

Back home Oyinmiebi found his father in the worst mood he had ever seen him in. The last time he had seen his father that grumpy must have been about a decade ago when Mr. Ovie, their oldest neighbor, had stormed into their house one morning to report that Oyinmiebi and some of his 'good-for-nothing friends' had stolen and roasted one of his chickens without even asking for his permission, as if he would have given it. That day not only had Oyinmiebi's father been grumpy and moody, the grumpiness occurred by seasonal trashing, too. Oyinmiebi very much doubted now if he was the cause of his father's bad mood and even if he was, he wondered if the 'old man' still had it in him to trash him now.

"Good evening father," he greeted. His father looked up at him from the newspaper in which he seemed engrossed and ignored the greeting. Oyinmiebi expected that. It was one of the things that went with his father's mood swings whenever he had them, so rather than taking offence and going on his way, Oyinmiebi sat on the chair next to his father and waited.

Oyinmiebi did not come from a rich family. He was a son of a fisherman. They were decent but poor, that much Oyinmiebi knew, and he was grateful to his father for having found a way to send him all the way to school despite the hardships they faced. As he sat beside his father on the hard thread-bare upholstered chair in their small and living room, he began to wonder how the man had managed to send him to school to study a course like law, when they struggled to meet a two-meal per day eating standard. His eyes went to the living room wall with faded paints. The walls in the living room used to be a touch of light-green. Now, seemed like the walls had no paint at all. Oyinmiebi did not want to think of how poor they were, but he couldn't help it. Acute fear gripped him every time he thought about it, and he felt so helpless. He often wondered how he would manage to enrol for law school if he didn't produce a plan to make money and fast. That was one reason why he didn't at all buy into Zuokumo's revolutionary spirit. He needed to find something decent to do and not stick around the bunch of Chief Oweila's fanatics. Oyinmiebi sighted a rat run pass a few yards from his feet and he couldn't help but smile. The sight was so usual to him now that sometimes he saw the mice as co-tenants in their two-bedroom run-down apartment. And compared to his cousin Zuokumo's living conditions, theirs were far better and much comfortable.

After waiting for a few more minutes Oyinmiebi decided to break the silence and find out what was wrong with his father.

"Please father, what is going on? I haven't seen you in such an awful mood in a long time," Oyinmiebi asked.

His father heaved a heavy sigh and closed the newspaper. The man was in his early fifties, but he looked much older, thanks to many years of hardship and challenging work.

"Have you been hearing, what has been going on?" he asked.

"About the on-going commotion with the sudden move of the new local government headquarters?"

"Exactly!"

"Yes papa, I have been hearing different stories and I must say they are most worrying," Oyinmiebi said, glad that he could talk about the issue with his quiet and reserved father.

"Most worrying? You have no idea how far this can go. Wait till the Itsekiris come and evict us from our homes claiming the land is theirs."

"Come on, father," Oyinmiebi held himself from laughing out loud.

"Sounds impossible now, but you wait. They claim the entire Warri belongs to them."

"Those are just unfounded claims. No proof whatsoever."

"Proof! Who even wants to see their proof anyway?

Nothing truthful comes out of that bunch of idiots."

"Well, they do have a lot of influence for sure," Oyinmiebi said not knowing if he was helping the matter at all.

"They were rejects from the Yoruba land who *we* allowed to settle here, because *we* let them have the land while *we* fished by the waterside, they say the entire land is theirs for the taking. As if that is not enough, they want to claim the entire hinterlands too." Oyinmiebi could see the bitterness in his father and he wished he shared that same bitterness, but he didn't. He just wanted peace enough to make sure he gets some business of some sort going, so he could start saving money for Law school. How did he come to think that he needed more adrenalin–pumping fun in his life? He wondered at what point he began to lose his way and he was glad he had set himself straight. It was hard enough to get just the full Nigerian Constitution into his brain, not to mention what he would still need to learn in Law School.

Dear Diary,

Okere Market is no more! Okere Market - where the women, and even the men of Warri, loved to come to buy the best things they would need to cook their best native soups, is no more.

As my driver and I approached the market from afar I could already see the black smoke rise to the sky, but I was not prepared to see what awaited me. Oh, it was a horrible thing to behold.

Our beloved Okere Market was in heaps of burning coals. I asked my driver to stop and turn back but it was too late. I had seen too much. Market women, men, girls, and boys ran about in utter chaos. Women screamed on top of their voices, for what, I had no idea. I could see fear. Fear in everybody's eyes. There was fear in my eyes too and my heart pounded. I grabbed the seat as Tega, my driver, tried to maneuver the car through the sudden rush of humans we ran into as we tried to rush back home.

I saw death face-to-face and even as life drained from my face, the faces that I beheld that day were faces I never wanted to see again.

I took one last look back at what used to be Okere market and a tear dropped from my eyes. Rows and rows of market stalls were still on fire and I could see boys throw buckets of water into it to stop the fire from spreading. Who could have done this? The Itsekiris? The Ijaws? The Urhobos? I was tired of the distinction and I was tired of the need to point accusing fingers at someone for every wrong done.

The car came to a screeching halt. I turned to see a mob gathering in front of my car. I screamed to Tega not to open the doors or windows for anyone. The boys in the mob began to hit on the bonnet hood of my car. I screamed and waved for them to get out of the road even as more fear gripped me. If I wasn't such a strong woman, at my age, I could had a heart attack.

The mob remained still and held us to a standstill.

Someone from amongst them stepped forward and ordered for us to wind down the car windows. I shook my head in refusal even as more tears began to roll down my cheek.

After what seemed like a good persuasion from the man who was the leader of the mob, Tega wound his side of the window just enough for him to hear the man speak. He demanded to know where we were headed, and I told him we were going back home. I told him we had come to the market to shop and then we saw the fires. Then he demanded to know what ethnic group I belonged to and I told him I was from Ibadan but married to an Urhobo man who passed away years ago. That didn't seem to move the man, but he was silent for a while. "Are you not an Ijaw woman?" The man asked. and I laughed out loud. I spoke with a distinctive Yoruba accent, and there were visible tribal marks on my face, unique only to the Yoruba people. "My son, I am originally from Ibadan, but you can consider me Urhobo now since I have been married to an Urhobo man for the past 50 years," I said. I could see the tension disappear from his face.

"Mama, the roads are not safe anymore. Please go home," he said and stepped aside. The mob did, too. I thanked him and heaved a sigh of relief as Tega put the car in motion.

What could have happened if I was from the 'wrong' ethnic group? Would they have beaten me to death? Burned me alive? Maimed me? I didn't want to think of it, because the thought itself enraged me.

If my children hear of what happened that day they would come and uproot me from this city, but I will not tell them. I am safe now and that is what matters. But is Warri safe? No! The city is under siege and I do not know where the next black smoke will rise from.

Tega hit the brakes again and I looked up, we were home.

Nine.

Tonye and Laju

A COLD RUSH OF MISTY BREEZE blew onto Laju's face as she stared out of the open window in her aunt's three-bedroom apartment somewhere in Ajamimogha just around the neighborhood from her grandmother's house. She had been staying there since she came into town with Tonye. She had chosen not to stay with her grandmother no matter how big the house was and no matter how hard the old woman had tried to convince her to stay. It was enough that grandmother was domineering even when not around her, let alone living under the same roof with her. It would have been like signing one's own death warrant. Laju closed her eyes, as if for a moment her father's voice would just drown away somewhere far from her but that was not possible now, was it? She could hear every word he said, and it was driving her crazy. She thought of Tonye and her heart leapt. They had made love just a few days ago. And Tonye had touched her in ways that he had never done before. But then Laju remembered that Tonye wasn't quite himself afterwards, just before she left. Looking back, she thought he was cold towards her.

What was wrong? Was he beginning to have doubts about their love? She dreaded the thought. She could still feel him inside her and her heart beat faster, making it harder to listen to what her father was saying. Not that it mattered; she knew he wasn't making much sense at all.

"Do you understand what I'm saying?" Her father's voice was a bit louder this time. That did the trick.

"Huh? No daddy, I do not understand. Why should I?" Laju rolled her eyes in irritation as her father's voice came from the other side of the line. The conversation was entering its second hour and they had been arguing over the same thing. She was getting weary of it all. Tears rolled down her eyes as she stared out the window and she wondered if she was crying or if something had blown into her eyes. She clutched the phone to her ears as if her very existence depended on it.

"But Daddy, I love him so much and you know that. You already met him twice and you admitted that you liked him. How can grandma change your mind just like that?" Laju sobbed.

"Your grandmother didn't convince me to do anything Laju," her father came again, this time sterner than before. He was getting angry because he had just realized that his daughter was so right. "All I am trying to say is to take it slow and not rush into a marriage you might end up regretting," he added.

"Daddy, can you hear yourself? I said *we* are ready. What more do you need to hear?"

Her father paused and Laju could hear the rise and fall of his heavy breathing, a result of a throat surgery he had undergone a few years ago. After what seemed like a few moments of pause, he heaved a sigh and continued but this time in a much lower and calmer tone.

"I do understand that you love Tonye and nobody is arguing about that, but it is not safe right now in Warri, so please I want you to come back to Lagos; let us talk about this as a family," he finished. Laju could imagine him rubbing his forehead as he always did when irritated but trying to keep a certain calm and poise.

"But Daddy…."

"Please Laju, could we not argue over this right now? I'm more worried about your safety than anything else."

"Dad, I can handle myself fine. I don't know why you worry so much."

"Laju, come home." And it was his final say.

"I will dad, in a few days."

"Extend my regards to your auntie. Bye for now, my dear."

Freezing wind rushed to Laju's face and she wished she was as free as the wind. Outside the window, she could see the short green grasses bow to the whims of the wind. She imagined herself as the grass and her grandmother as the strong willful wind. She wished she could break free now and run. Run as far away as she could. She was free once, when she was in the UK; before she met and fell in love with Tonye. She was free once upon a time, when she could walk down the street with the man she loved and tell everyone who cared to listen, 'Hey, this is my boyfriend.' She was free once; or was she? They never should have come to Nigeria. But was she ever 'away' from home? She may have been in the UK all those years, studying, but she was never free. Now, she wished she was. She hugged herself as the cold sent a chill down her spine.

Just then she felt a warm hand rest on her shoulder and she turned to investigate the smiling face of her beautiful aunt. Laju let go of herself and all the tears she had tried so hard to hold in began to flow. She threw herself into her auntie's warm embrace and sobbed in the woman's bosom. Her sobs were so heavy that she shook both herself and her auntie, who had a lean frame. Her aunt rubbed her back and whispered gentle and kind words into her ears.

"My darling, everything will be alright. Come and sit with me," the woman said, pulling Laju away and cleaning her eyes with the handkerchief she had with her. Laju obeyed and went to sit by her auntie.

"My dear, I can imagine what you must be going through right now, but we live in tough times. Love is not always what it seems," Auntie Eyitemi said and Laju turned to look at her face. She had not expected that from her auntie. At least not those exact words anyway.

What was going on? Had she heard wrong? Was this the same auntie of hers who ran off with her Igbo boyfriend to America to get married against the will of her family, bearing him three children? Was she the same auntie of hers who would tie herself to a tree in Manhattan during her school days to save it from lumberjacks, so the industrialists could build themselves yet another parking facility? Was she the same woman she admired and loved and emulated so much? There may be no one on her side at that moment, but Laju never would have thought that Auntie Eyitemi would object, too.

"Auntie I don't understand. I thought you understood and supported me," Laju said, trying not to show her disappointment in her shaky voice and control her sobs.

"I do understand my darling, and I do support you. But love and marriage are not something we jump into, on impulse."

"But Auntie, you eloped with your boyfriend to America."

Auntie Eyitemi chuckled and shook her head as if to shake away memories that she didn't what to remember.

"That was about three decades ago, and I do not regret it for one day, but my dear we live in a society where we have to uphold certain values."

"I love Tonye very much auntie and I want to marry him," Laju felt heartbroken. She felt betrayed.

"Of course, I do support you and Tonye. If I didn't, I would be a fool. The boy loves you."

"But why wait?"

"You, my darling, grew up in a protected world all your life. Outside these walls we have built around you kids is the harsh world."

"Harsh world? Auntie, I have lived away from home; away from Nigeria for years. I think I can very well handle myself."

"I'm sure you can but in as much as I do not agree with your grandmother and her 'iron' ways, you and Tonye should take things slow and get the full blessings from your family before you go on ahead."

"But auntie, you didn't get grandma's 'blessings' but you turned out fine."

"Yeah I did indeed but see how things turned out between me and 'them.' I mean your grandmother never speaks to me. My own mother, who happens to live just a short drive down from here. And your father and my other siblings take her side once it comes down to it."

"Don't say that auntie."

"But it is true. I'm fine with it anyway. I have my children to think about. And I'm sure my husband will be smiling down at me now from heaven seeing how well we have done without him being here with us."

Laju was silent while Auntie Eyitemi spoke. She watched the tears form in the woman's eyes and as they came down one streak after another. But the funny thing was, she was still smiling even as the tears came rolling. Laju felt so much for her. She was her favourite auntie. They had always shared a special bond right from when she was a little girl. Auntie Eyitemi was always the one who had the contrary view from everyone else's. It was because she was considered the black sheep of the family *who had eloped with an Igbo 'worthless boy' doing business in Onitsha market*, a fact grandmother never ceased to make clear whenever she had the chance. But see how they turned out. If not for the plane crash that took Uncle Emeka seven years ago, Auntie Eyitemi's marriage was one to emulate and it was always in grandma's face but that didn't stop the old woman from showing her disapproval whenever she wanted to.

"*Now* is what is wrong; the terrible times in which we live, my dear," Auntie Eyitemi's voice brought Laju back to reality. "You should talk to Tonye about going back to Lagos as your father instructed."

"Ok ma. I will talk to Tonye about it."

"Come here, my darling," Auntie Eyitemi said opening her arms. Laju rushed into her warm embraced and they were silent.

Another rush of cold misty breeze blew in from the window and both women held on to each other even tighter. Both women held on still as the cold began to grow within the room; one young and without the experiences of the other who was older and filled with life's stories. But the warm embrace they both shared showed how strong the bond they shared was and how great was the understanding they had of love's battles that lie ahead.

*

Tonye stepped on the brakes so hard, that he thought the car would flip over as he ran into a huge crowd that had appeared in the middle of the road as he drove back home from yet another meeting with Chief Warebi and Jolomi. Somehow the other men had taken their stands on which side they belonged to in the 'war' and they had stopped coming for the meetings. It was funny how fast they tagged the whole situation a 'war.'

He drove off the road and parked the car. He came down, secured the locks, and walked up to meet a few people that were gathering at a corner just close to the crowd.

"Hello, please what is happening?" Tonye asked. They turned to look at him with such looks that said, 'have you been living on the moon?' One of them volunteered to answer, or he was the fastest to speak because it seemed they all were ready to fill him in.

"*They* have just confirmed it, Warri South-West local government headquarters is in Ogidigben," the one woman in the group of five spoke. Tonye could hear the anger in her voice.

"Oh? When did this happen?" He asked.

"Shuoooo!!!! This morning o. After raising our hopes high that it would be in Ogbe-Ijoh," one of the other four men said.

"Haven't the Itsekiris taken enough from us? This must end o!"

"So where is the crowd headed?" Tonye continued.

"They are protesting na. Why are you asking questions as if you are a stranger? Or are you one of the Itsekiri spies?" Another of the four men spoke. The very sound of his voice carried enough violence for Tonye to think carefully before the next few words come out of his mouth.

"Ah!! No o, I'm Ijaw from Ezebiri. But I don't live here in Warri. I just came in," he said with a frozen smile of his face.

"Oh. Okay. Anyway, they are protesting. I think they are going to show the Itsekiris who is the boss in this Warri," the woman added and turned away. Soon the men did the same. Tonye took that as a cue to be on his way. He thought of Laju. *I think they are going to show the Itsekiris who is the boss in this Warri.* He remembered the woman's words. Laju was staying at her auntie's place right in the middle of one of the largest Itsekiri settlements in the city. Although the place was like a fortress, he just could not be sure of what could go wrong. Things were getting worse and he knew that for sure. He already knew the location of the new local government's headquarters even before anyone else because Chief Warebi had told them about it a few days ago in one of their meetings and he told them to be prepared for the worse. It was painful how trivial matters could soar to grand issues.

He got into his car after the road cleared and stepped on the accelerator as he raced down towards Ajamimogha, where Auntie Eyitemi's house was. He didn't think. He just drove. Or rather, all he could think about was seeing the face of the woman he loved and holding her in his arms and telling her how much he loved her.

He took the left turn heading into Ajamimogha road and stopped. Right ahead of him, miles ahead, he could see it.

Clear as day.

Visible.

Black smoke rose to the sky.

His heart stopped beating for a few seconds as blood rushed to his brains. His nose became runny. Once again, he came down from his car and crossed over to the other side of the road. He asked a few people what was happening even though he already knew the answer and the answer was simple: the war had started and there was no certainty who had dealt the first blow. Tonye knew from the distance of the house on fire that it was neither Auntie Eyitemi's nor grandmother Dawson's house, but the thought dreaded him, and he wanted to see Laju more now than ever. His legs shook. He got back into his car and somehow rather than continuing to Auntie Eyitemi's house, he turned around and headed for his house. Later, he would wonder why he did that. Was it shame? The shame that a war had broken out and that he was from one side of it, whether he had chosen a side or not, and on the other side was the woman he wanted to spend the rest of his life with? He felt guilty, even though he knew he shouldn't.

Tonye got back home an empty man. And as he slumped on his bed, his head filled with dreadful thoughts, he had a sick feeling. He wanted to see Laju, if just to reassure her that he didn't mean to act cold towards her the last time they were together. He longed to hold her in his arms again, to kiss her, to marry her, to make love to her, to…

He jumped up to his feet and ran back to his car. He headed down to Auntie Eyitemi's place, whether he liked it or not.

Ten.

Mogha and Seye

THE SILENCE THAT FOLLOWED was intense. Seye looked at the blood on his hands and looked at his brother.

"Seye are you alright?" Mogha asked. Shock written all over his face.

"Yes I am. Are *you* alright?" Seye returned the question, widening his eyes.

"Of course, I am. Why shouldn't I be?"

"B--because it's not my blood," Seye replied looking at the blood on his hands as if trying to make sure it was indeed not his and then at the bullet wound on his brother's left shoulder, "it's yours," he added.

Mogha placed a hand on his wounded left shoulder and winced.

"I'll be damned," he muttered under his breath.

"Let me have a look at it. Does it hurt?" Seye asked.

"I'm fine. The bullet must have grazed me or

something. It's just a scratch," Mogha said but it was more than a scratch. The bullet had gone right through his left shoulder missing the vital arteries there.

"It's a pretty big scratch bro, and it's letting out a lot of blood," Seye sounded panicky.

"Hey, calm down, will you. I said I'll be fine. In the meantime, we need to look for a way to get the hell out of here right now before these bastards get us."

Mogha tore the sleeve of his shirt and wrapped it around his wound without the help of his brother. At least that should stop the bleeding. Seye remained silent as he watched his brother attend to himself. He wanted to help but somehow, he found that he could not move himself. The noise coming from the mob outside was getting louder and increased rocks were being thrown at the house, a lot of which broke through their thick windows and landed right within the house. Some were just a few feet away from where the brothers were crouching.

"What did we do to them?" Seye began to say and Mogha looked at him.

"Shut the fuck up man. I don't need you to be a sissy now, you hear me? I need you to be fucking strong," he said and left him. Still crouched and on all fours, he crawled and went for the briefcase and the letter from their father. He returned to his brother to see that he had buried his head in his hands, weeping. He touched his shoulder and Seye looked up.

"I'm sorry for speaking to you like that, man. We need to get out of here, and I need you to be strong to do that."

"I'm sorry bro. But they killed Uncle Preye," Seye said still sobbing.

"I know man. I know," Mogha tried to be strong and he knew that sooner than later he would break, and he needed at least one of them to be strong and get them through this.

"Wait, can you smell that?" Seye asked.

"What's that?"

"I smell smoke."

"Fuck. The fire must be spreading into the house."

"Shit. We have to move" Seye was sounding more determined this time, more than ever.

Mogha acted fast. He jumped up, his wounded and bloodied arm limp by his side, and headed for the door. Seye crawled to join him. They opened the door leading to the corridor from where they could see past the stairs down into the large living room and had their fears confirmed. Their living room was on fire.

"Jesus!!!" Seye screamed.

"Fuck! Quick, we must move. The fire has not spread far," Mogha said and headed for the staircase. He didn't need to look back to see if Seye was following, his brother was at his heel and he could feel his heavy breath on the nape of his neck. The heat that enveloped the house came fast and the boys watched first-hand as the curtains their older sister picked and put up just a few months back disintegrated into nothingness. The heat acted even faster than the fire itself and it was just a matter of seconds before the brothers began to choke.

Mogha's wounded arm felt too heavy for him to carry along with him. His vision was becoming too blurred for him to know if he was taking one step after another on the long flight of stairs down to the living room or if he was falling through an abyss. Funny he still held on to the gun. Both their lives depended on it. He began to turn around to make sure Seye was still right behind him, to ask his brother if he was okay.

To remind him to be strong.

To tell him to be a man.

To reassure him that everything would be fine.

To apologize to him for calling him a sissy even after he had promised he would never call him that or any other slur for that matter after Seye had confessed to him in London that he fancied boys to girls.

But nothing was coming out of his mouth. He wasn't even sure if he was saying anything. He saw Seye in double as his vision began to fail him.

Seye had never been so afraid in his entire life. Yes, he was a spoilt child. Yes, he had had everything handed to him just by asking for it. Yes, he would admit that he grew up weak and fragile like an ancestral egg that no one must touch. Yes, he looked up to his brothers who in turn did everything for him. But today he knew he had to forget all of that and stand firm. As he walked behind Mogha in the growing heat from the fire, he noticed that his brother was swaying and the blood from his wounded hand was dripping down his hand and onto the floor leaving behind a terrible trail. He rushed to him just before he fell and toppled over on the stairs. The heat was unbearable.

"Come on Mogha, open your eyes," Seye said but Mogha did not respond. He just kept moving one foot after another climbing down the stairs like a puppet.

There was no noise coming from outside the house now. The mob had left, feeling victorious. All Seye could hear were the crackles of the wood from the windows now on fire. He felt a scratch in his throat and he coughed. And he coughed again. And again. And then he knew he was choking and so was Mogha.

The strength came from nowhere. It had been within him all along and he just didn't know it or perhaps the extremity of the heat jump-started something in his brain that woke him up, he would never know, Seye just acted. Mogha slumped to the hot ground as they got to the base of the long flight of stairs and onto the living room which was now very much ablaze. Sweat flowed from their faces as if a faucet turned on within them.

Seye didn't look around at their once beautiful living room. Or at their Italian leather chairs now melting away from the heat. Or at the huge flat screen Sony television their father had bought all the way from Australia. Or at their pictures on the wall all cracked and bent out of place.

Seye didn't think of the life he was leaving behind, he thought of the life he and his brother may not have at all, if he didn't do something and fast.

"The kitchen. Back door," Mogha's voice came like a

sound from within Seye's head but Seye knew Mogha had spoken and he was glad because it was a sign that he was still breathing.

"Are you alright?" Seye asked as he threw his brother's good right arm over his shoulder. Mogha held on to the shotgun. Mogha did not need to answer the question. Seye knew. They limped and struggled in the growing heat, their skin felt like it was melting off their backs, but they were in the kitchen in no time. The fire was spreading fast now.

The kitchen back door was another war in front of them. The door had not seen use in such a long time that the boys couldn't even remember the last time. The padlocks which secured the door had both rusted and fused together. Their father had stopped them from using the back door because he didn't want them or anyone else for that matter sneaking into his house, he had said.

"Fuck!" Seye muttered. He rested Mogha on the kitchen cabinet and rushed for the concrete grinder of the local, little-used grinding stone. He hit the first padlock several times before it gave way. The second wasn't half as difficult. He grabbed the gun from Mogha and aimed at the lock on the door itself and fired. The door shifted and gave in.

They both lost their hearing. All they could hear now were muffled sounds.

Seye gave the door one hard kick and the door flew open outwards. He went back to his brother and helped him up. Seye peered out first to see if anyone was outback but the area was clear.

The boys stepped out of their house - now very much on fire and breathed in fresh air.

"Come on bro; let's get the hell out of here," Seye said as he held Mogha's hand around his shoulder and helped him as they found their way from their back yard towards the little back gate on the fence. Seye feared taking Mogha through the front for fear that the mob might still be there.

Luck seemed to be on their side, because the back gate remained unlocked.

Seye had gotten rid of the gun as they began their trek towards Airport Road. Mogha seemed a bit relaxed now because he was speaking. The sight both the brothers beheld was unbelievable. When they had come in from the airport, it was raining heavily, and the town was peaceful, but now they saw utter chaos. Black smoke rose to the sky from everywhere they looked. People were running helter-skelter, screaming and wailing in words that the boys could not understand. People had loads and Ghana-must-go bags on their heads heading out to God-knows-where and they didn't look like they were coming back. It was clear; they were running away from home just like them.

Seye thought of asking a few questions but he just didn't think it was necessary. He needed to get himself and his brother out of there and Mogha needed a hospital.

The first *okada* he hailed down refused to stop and so did a million others after. Mogha was groaning now and they had been walking for about thirty minutes now.

At last, Seye got a rider to stop.

"Take us to General Hospital and I'll give you one hundred US dollars," Seye said before the *okada* rider could open his mouth to say anything in protest. The man swallowed whatever it was he wanted to say and said instead, "Ok, show me."

"Seye opened the briefcase and was trying to withdraw a note when the man added, "give me a bunch and I'll take you."

Seye didn't protest. He withdrew the whole bunch and gave it to the man as he helped him put Mogha on the motor bike. Seye joined behind his weakened older brother and held on to him as the bike got into motion.

There were no more words exchanged between the boys and the *okada* rider. He took them straight to the over-crowded Warri General Hospital, dropped them off, and went on his way having benefited from the misfortune of another. He must have been thankful to the gods for giving him such a fruitful day.

Seye screamed on the top of his lungs for a stretcher as soon as they were off the motor bike. Two nurses rushed to them with a stretcher and helped Mogha onto it.

"Who is on call?" Seye heard one of them ask the other.

"Never mind who is on call Sarah. Get Dr. Toju. She's a volunteer for all the war victims. She has been on call since *it* started," the latter said.

That was when it dawned on Seye. They were in the

middle of a war. But who was at war with whom? Seye just could not understand it. He held on to his brother's good hand as they rushed him into the hospital and with his other hand, he clutched the briefcase. He had to keep it safe; at least it would buy them their tickets back to the UK and Seye knew he was never coming back to Warri. Never again!

Eleven.

Toritseju and Jolomi

TORITSEJU WOKE UP ALONE in bed that morning. It was something she adjusted to these days. It didn't bother her anymore except for the fact that she was worried sick for her husband's safety. Jolomi was never around now. When he came home, it would be to eat something and then he would be off again, camera at hand, ready to shoot what he described as the greatest news-worthy story ever to come out of the Delta region and even Nigeria. And in the dead of night when he came home to bed, she would be so fast asleep – tired from the work-load she had in the hospital – that she wouldn't even hear him come in or feel his presence in bed. It'd been three days now since Jolomi came home dishevelled and showed her graphic images on his digital camera of the violence taking place in the Ijaw and Itsekiri hinterlands which nobody seemed to be aware of, and she feared that it was a matter of time before the violence spread into the city. Already she had treated so many burn cases in the hospital all related to this inter-ethnic crisis. And now that the news was everywhere, that the new local government's headquarters were

Ogidigben. She could only stand prepared for the worse.

Shower and breakfast were quiet and uneventful. There wasn't the usual chatter she and Jolomi used to have just before they left for work. There wasn't the occasional foreplay and quick kitchen sex they used to enjoy just while she prepared breakfast. There wasn't Jolomi's usual tardiness for her to clean up after. There was nothing, just a sick feeling of emptiness and fear. Her mind filled with so many thoughts that she could not think straight. She was like a zombie.

Toritseju often wondered what was missing in her life, all those years ago when she was much younger, all through her days in Medical School in New York, until she met and fell in love with Jolomi. That singular event changed everything. That gave her a purpose to live. Jolomi was a damaged man who needed fixing and there she was, so she took on the quest to fix him. Now she didn't quite feel that way anymore. She found herself slipping away, as if falling into a chasm with no way back and it was such a scary and sickening feeling to have all over again. She needed to get out of the house and breathe in some fresh air.

Toritseju had just left their apartment to look for a taxi to the hospital when it happened.

Boom! Came the first sound and that was enough to register.

It happened so fast, and she just stood there, shaking and frozen.

And then, fire. It was everywhere.

Toritseju may not have found the strength to lift her feet if she hadn't seen the rush of people who had appeared from around the corner.

Running. Wild. Angry, and then afraid.

She too broke into a wild run. Her breath left her too many times, but she found a way to get it back as she ran, clutching her handbag under her armpit.

Jolomi and Toritseju lived in an area in Warri populated by the Ijaws. Everyone had been against the idea of them living so close to an opposing ethnic group but Jolomi was not one to hear of it. He was a radical and the prospect of living amongst the Ijaws was a challenge he awaited. Now, as Toritseju ran towards safety, where she'd find it - she had no idea, she longed for Jolomi and prayed for his safe return to her wherever he might be.

Toritseju was lucky to find a taxi driver willing to stop amid the commotion.

"General Hospital," she said to the taxi driver amidst her panting as she jumped into the back of the car. As she tried hard to catch her breath, she looked back and saw the thick black smoke rising to the sky. Toritseju did not know when tears began to roll down her face. She knew she wouldn't be able to get back home. Not now. Life there was over, and the war just came to her doorstep. She thought of Jolomi. Where could he be? God! She prayed for his safety and for him to have the common sense to know that he cannot change everything. She buried her face in her palms and sobbed like she had never done before. Warri was under siege.

*

Jolomi looked down at his beautiful wife as she slept. He could imagine the dreams she was having. Did she dream of them having a better life surrounded by better circumstances or did she dream that she had never met him; maybe then her life wouldn't be so complicated? He didn't know. But from the peaceful look on her face, Jolomi knew his wife was happy in her dreams and that was all that mattered. He reached forward to touch her smooth almond-shaped face but stopped in mid-action. He didn't want to wake her up that morning or all the earlier mornings before that whenever he left for *work*. There was so much to do and so little time to get it all done. He snuck out of bed and into the shower. The water was cold. NEPA had done their magic: no electricity and so the heater was not working. He managed with the icy water, which he was getting quite used to anyway and had a quick shower.

Toritseju was still fast asleep when he planted a kiss on her forehead and left the house without asking her if he could drop by at the hospital to take some photo shots of victims of the war.

It was 5am. Armed with his NIKON digital camera, a small SONY camcorder and a tape recorder, he walked for a while down the Okumagba Layout road before he saw an *okada*. The rider stopped even before he flagged him down; they had a way of doing that.

Jolomi tried to enjoy the breeze as he rode on the back of the motor bike to NPA waterside where he would catch his waiting boat, but he knew that the breeze would be short-lived. He could not get the last message he got from Chief Warebi off his head. The chief was in hiding somewhere safe, and he was advised to let go of his pursuit for stories about the Warri crisis since things seemed to have taken a bad and violent turn and keep away from the violence. With a vast number of deaths already recorded and landed properties worth millions from both warring parties already lost, there was no use being allegiant now. One had to think of one's own safety. Those were the words of the chief. But something else the chief had said roused his curiosity and quest for the perfect story even more. The chief had admitted having heard from a reliable source that there was a dialogue between Ijaw and Itsekiri leaders to reach an agreement which included sharing the offshore oil revenue from oil derived from the village of Angbarama on the Escravos River south of Warri and other villages with crude oil flow stations located in them. No way was Jolomi going to let that slide without checking it out.

Therein rested his quest. He needed to confirm the story and for the last time finish his story and send on to CNN. He was so excited about it.

Having posed as a university student out to do research on the mangroves of the Escravos River, Jolomi had been able to secure an interview with one of the aides of the traditional ruler in Angbarama. The boat ride from NPA waterside to the village was smooth, during which time Jolomi took pictures and enjoyed the maneuvering of the motor-boat on the Escravos River.

Cold and salty water splashed on Jolomi's face and he remembered the last time he and Toju went on vacation on one of the beautiful beaches of Lagos. It was wonderful. He wished they could relive those days again. Those days, when being in love was worth everything in the world. He wished he could go back to the time when he could always make her smile; when his jokes made sense to her and when they both just couldn't wait to get back home and make love.

Jolomi looked up into the light-blue sky as dawn broke and as the awakening sun smiled down on earth from beyond the horizons of the thick bluish clouds up above in the sky. He smiled at the beauty and constancy of nature; at how all things seemed to enjoy such a wonderful connection. He smiled as he looked down into the river, at the thick ripples of waves caused by the propeller of the motorboat and at the fish that jumped up on occasions to enjoy a bit of oxygen and catch a glimpse of whoever it was that was disturbing its peaceful existence. He looked across to the dense mangroves on the far end of the river banks and wondered what form of life was lurking within it. Jolomi had a way of letting his mind wonder about such things. That was why he was such a great journalist in the first place.

Soon the sun would come out just as it had done the day before and the day before that but there they were, humans killing each other over a piece of land. He caught the gaze of one of the passengers and nodded a silent greeting to him. The man returned the nod and turned to look away. Jolomi wondered what his story was. He was a husband, a father, a son, and a brother. Jolomi wondered what quests he was pursuing; he wondered what dreams he had. He wondered why he was on that boat that morning. Well, he would never know. The man had his gaze fixed into the dense mangroves as the boat slowed down. Jolomi looked around him, they were approaching a village. This must be Angbarama. Why else would the boat driver be preparing to dock?

Jolomi picked up his backpack and wore it on his back as he waited for the boat to dock by the side of the river. He got off and nodded a farewell greeting to the man he had nodded a greeting earlier to as the man went on his way.

Jolomi spent a good three hours roaming about the village, taking pictures, and gathering information about how to get to the traditional ruler's palace. Everywhere looked peaceful. No one even cared or acted like they noticed a strange man taking photos of their village. They just went on with their lives. They didn't seem to care that there was no electricity in the village. Or that they didn't have televisions in their little huts – that is, if they knew what the magic box was for anyway. They didn't seem to mind that many barrels of crude oil pumped from beneath the ground they walked on; from within the river they went to shit from the edge of their hand-crafted canoes. Perhaps they thanked the gods for sending the '*good people*' of Shell or Chevron or Elf for '*helping them*' dispose of '*the black demon shit*' which had been polluting their waters and farmlands for so long. Jolomi just could not understand how a village which was the site for that huge amount of crude oil could not enjoy a simple amenity like electricity. Nonetheless, Jolomi still admired the serenity they enjoyed. He admired their ignorance. It is said, 'what one doesn't know wouldn't harm him.' He wished he and Toritseju were there together, away from all the hustle of Warri and the constant fear of the unknown. Everyone there in the village didn't seem affected by what was happening on the other side of the river or in neighbouring villages raided by the Itsekiri militia.

As the sun set up shop far up in the sky, Jolomi began to head out for the king's palace. *The Pere,* the traditional rulers in most Ijaw villages, was *indisposed* to see him or he just didn't want to give an interview, so Jolomi was making do with the willing aide. The aide would, of course, love to see his name in Jolomi's 'mangrove reports' when it would be published in 'The National Environmental Gazette' – lies Jolomi had so fed him to let him do the interview.

The Pere's palace was a modern structure, as opposed to most of the mud huts Jolomi had met in his roaming around in the village. And the palace also enjoyed electricity. Every light bulb shone, so bright that Jolomi shielded his eyes from their blazing glow. Jolomi could hear the huge generator coming from somewhere within the massive palace. Parked in a garage were three exotic cars. There wasn't even a road leading to the village yet. The Pere had two beautiful Mercedes and a BMW for his *viewing pleasure.* Jolomi laughed.

As Jolomi waited in a room that smelled like dead wood, he prepared his questions in his head. The high chief would be disappointed when he'd switch from talks about their mangroves to crude oil business.

"High Chief Tamaraebi will see you now. Please

follow me," the middle-aged man who had attended to him when he first arrived, said, emerging from the door he had disappeared into.

"It's about time," Jolomi said under his breath.

Jolomi followed the pot-bellied middle-aged man as he led him in silence to see the High Chief. At the door, the palace attendant knocked and after a short while he opened the door. Jolomi didn't hear a voice from within urging them to come in so he figured that was customary for them. The High Chief sat behind his desk when Jolomi came in. He didn't look up from the book he was reading neither did he speak to the attendant when he greeted him. Instead he waved his hand and the attended, taking that as his cue, left Jolomi alone with the High Chief. Jolomi stood there for a minute. He didn't know if he should offer himself a seat or get angry at the fact that the High Chief also did not respond to his earlier greeting when he walked in.

After what felt like an embarrassing time in front of your high school principal, the High Chief looked up at Jolomi and offered him a seat with a nod towards one of the empty chairs in front of him.

Jolomi sat down and brought out his tape recorder and notepad.

Five minutes into the interview, after Jolomi had asked his phony questions, he posed the real one, bringing up the rumors he's heard that led him to that village in the first place.

The High Chief flared up.

"How dare you accuse His Royal Highness of

conniving with those Itsekiri scoundrels to divide crude oil revenue? That is a – um – preposterous accusation for you to – um – make, young man!" The high chief blared, the moment Jolomi brought up the main purpose for his visit.

"I didn't throw any accusations sir. I just asked you to confirm a rumour."

"Confirm a rumour? Are you – um – mad?"

"No sir I am not," Jolomi was trying hard to hold his contempt and anger even as the high chief shouted and rained saliva at him.

"Then why would you expect me to – um – confirm a story that is not – um – true? Mr. Man, I think it's time for you to leave," the chief shouted.

"Thank you for your time. I'll be sure to describe His Royal Highness's cars in my report," Jolomi said, and was standing up when the middle-aged palace servant rushed into the high chief's office without even knocking. He began to scream and say something in Ijaw that Jolomi could not understand.

"I suggest you leave at once, young man," the high chief added as he began to rush out of the room on the heels of the servant.

Jolomi threw his things into his backpack and jumped to his feet and ran after them.

"What's going on sir?" he asked as he caught up with the high chief and the servant at the palace gates.

"Please leave young man. For the sake of your safety."

"But what is going on?"

"Itsekiri boys are coming!!!" the servant shouted as they appeared from the palace and Jolomi could not believe what met his eyes. The peaceful village he had walked through only that morning before the sun came out flew into a huge turmoil as everyone ran for their dear lives and into hiding. For some reason Jolomi could not understand, he looked up into the sky and thick dark clouds were beginning to gather and shield the rays of the sun from reaching the earth.

From afar, Jolomi could hear sounds of heavy gunshots, fired into the air to announce their presence. He retrieved his camera, tightened the strap of his backpack on his back and began to run. He wasn't running away. He wasn't going into hiding. He was heading for the banks of the river. The very dock from whence he had come into the village. The militia would come in from there, too. As Jolomi reached the river banks, he looked up far into the Escravos River, and he counted them. One, two, three, four, he lost count when he got to eight. That was the number of motor boats that came to drop off the boys who were coming for the rumoured 'peaceful' dialogue.

They were armed. Firing their guns into the sky. Fast approaching.

And then time stood still. The gods must have been retiring to bed now.

Twelve.

Oyinmiebi

HOT TEARS STUNG OYINMIEBI'S EYES as they gathered. He held on to the blunt machete in his right hand. What was he going to do with it? He had no idea. The deed had already occurred. Right in front of him stood empty and bare, the place where his cousin Zuokumo's house used to be. In its place was a pile of rubble. A pile of shattered hopes and broken dreams. A huge pile still smoky from the fiery storm it could not have withstood. He watched as people ran, scattered like dry leaves being blown away. He watched as women cried out in tears for their missing children, their worn-out wrappers falling from their waists, not caring to pick them up or cover their nakedness. He watched as children searched for their mothers, all covered in dirt and blood. He stood there, powerless and defeated as wives mourned the death of their husbands, and as husbands mourned the loss of their livelihood and source of income. He stood there and watched as the venom from the attack spread so fast that he wished he wasn't just standing there and doing nothing.

What was he to do?

They had come fast, and from all sides. They had filled the little community, pouring in like hordes of bees, stinging everyone and everything on their path. Oyinmiebi stood there as the tears finally began to roll down his face and it all came back to him.

He and Zuokumo had had an intense argument about the latter's involvements in the Ijaw militia. He had called his cousin a low-life and a trigger-happy murderer who derived pleasure from preying on the 'innocent.' Now, he wished he hadn't said all those things to him.

"And who do you think you are, a saint?" Zuokuma had screamed back at him at the top of his lungs and vibrating from so much anger and a struggle to put it in check.

The argument had gone on for a long time before Oyinmiebi stormed out of his cousin's house and had taken a long walk down the shore of the Ogbe-Ijoh waterfront. He was about to turn around and head back to Zuokumo's when he had seen her.

Faith!

She had appeared like a ghost, hunting him from his past and she looked even more beautiful than ever. Oyinmiebi recognized her in an instant. He was shocked and impressed to see that she hadn't changed much from what she used to look like when she was fifteen, when he had last seen her. They looked the same age now. Oyinmiebi was a bit sad to have heard that she had just gotten married to some rich man from Australia a few months back. But now he was so glad to see her.

Faith was walking past him, not recognizing who he was, when he called her name.

She had turned in surprise. Her face without a smile.

"I'm sorry but my name is Oyinmiebi Ebielador, you may not recognize…." He watched her face light up in an instant. She did remember.

"Oh, my goodness. Oyinmiebi? Little Oyinmiebi, my little husband?" She exclaimed rushing towards him. Oyimiebi blushed so hard the redness was almost visible on his chocolate-toned face. He had a wide grin, so wide that for a moment he forgot all the sorrows in the world.

"Yes, it is me," he said as she grabbed him in an embrace.

"Oh my God, it has been a lifetime Oyinmiebi. How have you been?" she said, releasing him from her tight embrace and looking into his face. Oyinmiebi felt the firmness of her breast on his chest. He just wished she hadn't noticed his heart quicken.

"I am great."

"Hmm... I hear you are now a young barrister," she teased.

"Actually, not yet. I'm yet to attend the Nigerian Law School."

"Oh, that is great Oyinmiebi. That is good."

"Well, it's nothing. It will be really tough, though."

"Of course, it would be," They were walking together down the shore now. "Nothing comes without hard-work, my young man," she said and smiled, revealing a clean set of dentitions.

Oyinmiebi wondered why he couldn't say all that he wanted to say. It was like his tongue sat tied somewhere within his mouth. He just kept nodding to all she said and smiling. He thought his head would explode because whenever he smiled too much, he got a pounding headache.

"Um—I heard you are now married," Oyinmiebi said and he saw the smile dwindle on her face the moment he spoke about her marriage.

"My dear, I am married but to be sincere, it doesn't feel like a marriage, because my husband is far away in Australia and I am still here filing papers to get a visa, so I can go and join him."

"I'm sorry to hear that."

"It is alright. It's just terrible what we have to go through to get a visa these days in this country."

Oyinmiebi agreed with a series of nods. He had not the slightest idea what people went through. He had never tried to get a visa before.

"Terrible times we are living in o. See what has been happening between these Ijaw and Itsekiri boys," she said slowing down to a stop. She held her hand to her chin in a distinctive thoughtful pose.

"It is terrible. They have raided so many Ijaw villages already. It's just terrible."

"Well, the Ijaw boys haven't been silent. We aren't safe here, you know. Here is where the war is coming."

"Why do you say that?" Oyinmiebi felt stupid to even ask.

"Why do I say so? But the cause of the so-called fight is because Ogidigben won over Ogbe-Ijoh for the new local government headquarters, is that not so? If anyone should be grieved it should be us."

"I hear our boys have invested so much in protecting this side."

"I sure hope so my dear. Anyway, I must run along now. My father is waiting for me at the pharmacy. Now that I am visiting, I should as well be the local doctor and not just the local chemist's daughter," she said and they both laughed.

"Ok. It is so great to see you again ma," Oyinmiebi said and Faith looked at him funny.

"It is great to see you too Oyinmiebi. But please call me Faith na. Where is the 'ma' coming from?" She said with a chuckle as she walked away.

Oyinmiebi felt the ground should open and embrace him and never let go. *It is so great to see you again ma.* How stupider could that have sounded. He hit his forehead as he headed back home.

*

Oyinmiebi slumped to the ground, letting go of his blunt machete as he sighted Zuokumo rushing towards him from a corner. His body covered in blood. Not his blood though. He had been active in fighting when the Itsekiri militia had attacked. He had fought like a man, the same man whom Oyinmiebi may have cuckolded with insults and undeserving misgivings.

Zuokumo began to say something but all Oyinmiebi could hear were muffled sounds like he was sitting by the engine of an airplane. It was not until he heard *her* name that he looked up at his cousin.

"What did you just say?" Oyinmiebi said, jumping to his feet.

Zuokumo refused to say more.

"What did you say about Faith? What about her?" Oyinmiebi asked.

Zuokumo released a huge sigh.

"I said we just found her. I'm sorry," Zuokumo said. He was a hard man and his face portrayed how bitter and hardened he had become.

Oyinmiebi felt his knuckles give way.

"How is she?" he asked, and prayed Zuokumo didn't give him an answer. He didn't need to speak; his expression told Oyinmiebi what he didn't want to hear.

"She had been raped and stabbed."

Oyinmiebi shut his ears with both his hands as his cousin began to give him gory details of the state in which Faith's body was.

Faith! His childhood crush. The same woman he had run into by the riverside only hours before the sudden attack. The same woman who had seemed so happy. The same woman who had just married a man Oyinmiebi was sure she loved with all her heart. The same woman who was a medical doctor and had a lot of life in her.

Oyinmiebi was surprised that tears had stopped flowing from his eyes. He felt so much rage that his body began to shake, and he did not know when Zuokumo grabbed him in a strong embrace and began to speak words into his ears. The only words that stuck in his brain from what Zuokumo was saying were 'retaliation attack,' 'protect other villages,' 'vengeance', 'revenge', 'let's go NOW'.

It was with that urgency that Oyinmiebi let go of all his beliefs in peace and went along with Zuokumo. Zuokumo had mentioned that they heard the Itsekiri boys were planning an attack on Angbarama so the Ogbe-Ijoh militia together with other Ijaw boys was planning a counter attack.

*

The Itsekiri boys had finished their attack on Angbarama and had disappeared into the high sea before they got there hours later. From their motor boats far within the Escravos River the boys watched in anguish as, yet another Ijaw village lay in waste; sacked and destroyed. A few boats floated towards the crude oil flow station found within the dense mangrove forest of the village, but they already knew there was nothing they could do to salvage it. They could already see the black smoke climbing like a fleet of black horses ascending into the sky, turning the day into night in an instant.

Oyinmiebi and Zuokumo went to comb the surrounding bushes around the village for survivors hiding within it and armed and ready in case they ran into any form of resistance. They had both received military-grade weapons. Where the weapons had come from, they both had no idea.

Oyinmiebi could not keep his head straight. He thought about everything at the same time. He thought about his life. He thought about his family, hiding with a vast number of others somewhere *safe* within the city of Warri; the same city that was also under siege. He thought of what his life could be like, if and after he survived this. He thought of Faith and how much he had loved her all his life even though he knew he never would have told her how he felt. He thought of everything.

Zuokumo was gathering together a few women and children hiding in the bushes telling them in Ijaw that they were there to 'save' them, as if that was true. Oyinmiebi broke away from him and the small group of people and moved further into the mangrove trees, silent and haunted by God-knows-what, buried within himself; a robot just walking without life. Just then, he heard rustles within the bushes. With his gun at the ready he approached where the sound was coming from.

There, lying on the muddy ground and covered in dirt and blood was a man with a backpack just as dirty and muddy strapped on his back. His body poured blood from a gunshot wound.

Oyinmiebi rushed to him and threw his gun on the ground as he fell to the ground to the man's aide.

"H---Help me!" The man whispered as blood sprouted from his mouth as he spoke.

"Shh! You will be alright. What is your name?" Oyinmiebi said in Ijaw.

The man shook his head.

"Journalist," The man managed again, getting weaker and weaker as he spoke.

"Jesus!" Oyinmiebi said under his breath as he looked around him on the muddy earth clueless of what he was looking for or what to do. The man kept trying to speak, but blood came out of his mouth. Oyinmiebi could hear him as he gasped for breath. He let out a horrible sound from his lungs, a sound that would haunt Oyinmiebi for the rest of his life.

"Bag!" The man said.

Oyinmiebi removed his backpack from his back and opened it. The contents within it were a camcorder, a digital camera, a tape recorder, a notepad, and a wallet. Oyinmiebi grabbed the wallet as he began to hear Zuokumo scream his name from afar. He opened the wallet and saw the man's Press ID bearing CNN on it. It was an old card, as he guessed from the young picture on it, but it was him. He looked at the name on the card, it read: Jolomi Daniel Benson. Oyinmiebi looked to make sure he was seeing right. He jumped to his feet and grabbed his gun pointing it at the helpless and unarmed man. Oyinmiebi's hands trembled, as different scenarios played in his mind.

Who was this mysterious man?

Was he a spy?

He was one of the Itsekiri soldiers attacked by villagers while trying to escape.

The man lifted his trembling hand in a bid to beg for

his life, but he seemed too weak to even keep his hand up long enough. It fell back to the ground.

Oyinmiebi lowered his weapon and returned to the man who was trying hard to talk, even though it was obvious he was in terrible pain.

"Were you part of the attack?" Oyinmiebi found himself asking as Zuokumo's voice calling his name drew closer. His cousin must be looking for him within the mangrove trees.

"…wife. Toju Benson. Show my wife," the man said and stopped moving.

"What are you…" Zuokumo stopped talking as he got to Oyinmiebi and saw what had been delaying him.

"He was just some village guy. Come on, let's get back," Oyinmiebi said standing up suddenly as Zuokumo began to get curious.

"What's in the bag?" Zuokumo asked, not fooled.

"The guy was a journalist, and these are his things."

"Have you seen what's inside?"

"Zuokumo, trust me on this. Let's get back to Warri and we will look through it together," Oyinmiebi said and began to walk away from Zuokumo and the dead man back into the village.

His cousin did not argue. He just walked behind him as they went back to join the rest of the wailing village. The villagers were re-emerging from their places of hiding as they began to mourn their losses. Oyinmiebi remembered Ogbe-Ijoh, but what happened there in

Angbarama was much worse than what they had seen in Ogbe-Ijoh. A few yards from where they stood was what used to be the traditional ruler's palace now up in flames and ruins.

Thirteen.

Tonye and Laju

LAJU RUSHED INTO TONYE'S ARMS the moment she saw him jump out of his car. He had arrived just on the nick of time. She was leaving Warri. The entire Dawson family was. Grandmother had made that clear when she had called an emergency meeting. The Dawson family was an open target, so she wanted them all to move until the insurgence died down and with the way the violence was growing no one knew when that would be.

"Oh my God, thank God you came. I have been trying to go look for you, but my auntie wouldn't let me leave," Laju said into Tonye's ears as she held him in a tight embrace.

Tonye held her.

"Are you leaving?" Tonye asked, as if the answer wasn't staring right back at him.

"We are fleeing the city, Tonye. It is not safe here for us," Laju said, finally releasing Tonye after long enough, that they had to catch their breath

"Has it come to this?"

"I'm afraid it has. My grandmother and most of our family members have already left and we have to too," Laju said.

Auntie Eyitemi appeared from the house dragging along with her a huge case. Tonye rushed to her aid as he saw her.

"How are you, Tonye?" Auntie Eyitemi said as Tonye took the case from her. She stood upright to take a better look at the man who wanted to marry her niece.

"Well, given all that has been happening in this brief time, I wish I could say I'm fine ma'am. But thank you for asking. So where are you going?" Tonye asked turning to face Laju.

"Benin City for now and then on to Lagos," Laju said.

Tonye's heart skipped a beat. He rushed back to where Laju was standing with her hands on her hips.

"Honey, Lagos? And you were just going to leave like that?"

Tonye's face registered nothing but pain.

"I told you I've been trying to reach you. Baby look around you, does it look like a place where we should be right now?"

"I know. Okay. I'll come with you," Tonye said.

Laju heaved a sigh and Tonye wondered what she was thinking about.

"Tonye, you can't just follow us right now. We are already leaving for Benin City."

"I'll drive behind you." Tonye felt like he was begging the woman he loved to let him go with her wherever she wanted to go and that made him feel awkward.

"Meet me in Benin City. But my entire family will be there. My grandmother would, too."

"So? Am I supposed to be afraid of them?"

"I didn't say that baby. I was just saying that, given what has been happening, it may not be an appropriate time to show up in front of my family."

"Why? Because I am Ijaw?" Tonye asked. He was angry now.

Laju was silent.

"Answer me," he said gritting his teeth, so he didn't raise his voice.

"Yes Tonye. Why else wouldn't they approve of our getting married? Ehn? Because you are Ijaw. And now see what is happening."

"Are you blaming me for all that is going on?" Tonye could not believe what he was hearing. Where was this coming from? Laju didn't sound like the woman he knew. She was nothing like the woman he had made love to what seemed like yesterday because he could still feel her sharp fingernails piercing into his back while they made love.

"Tonye, how could I blame you for all this? Who do I even blame? Last night my Uncle's house burned. I didn't want to say anything about it but there you have it."

It was Tonye's turn to be silent. The next time he spoke, he was calmer.

"I'm sorry. Things have indeed been crazy. But I will be in Benin City tomorrow Laju, and I don't care what your family thinks," Tonye said as he took her hands and squeezed them.

Tears rolled down Laju's face.

"Tonye, we have a lot to talk about, but now is not the time," Laju said as she struggled with one hand to fight the tears on her face.

"What are you talking about?" Tonye feared the worst.

"Laju come on, it's time," Auntie Eyitemi called from beside the car, which was running.

"Tonye, we have to go now. Wait, let me write down the address and a number to reach me on," Laju said rushing to the car and to her handbag. She brought out a small stick-on pad and wrote down the address and phone number of where she would be and handed it to Tonye. She gave him one last hug before she got into the car.

"I love you, Tonye," she said.

"I love you, too." Tonye stood there, rooted to the ground as he watched the car drive away with the woman he loved.

He went back into his car and broke into tears. He feared so many things, more than he thought he could handle. How did it ever come to this? He wished he could turn back the hands of time. He wished he could go all the way back to when he and Laju were in the UK.

They should have just gotten married out there, rather than chase traditions all the way home and for what, to be disappointed and judged.

Tonye looked down at the piece of paper in his hand, it felt heavy to carrying the sheet and he felt it was the end. Laju didn't sound like the woman he had fallen in love with. She sounded different, adulterated and changed. Her family had succeeded in changing her mind. He did not care. He loved her from the depths of his heart, and he was ready to go to the ends of the earth until he found her.

Tonye started his car and headed home. He needed to park. There was no point staying in the city. Chief Warebi had already told him and Jolomi to go somewhere safe so Tonye didn't plan on wasting more time in the desolate city; he had to be on his way to Benin City.

*

Laju remained silent beside Auntie Eyitemi as the driver sped on through the city of Warri as he made his way towards the exit of the city. It was real. Warri was no more. Laju had lost count of the number of houses that had already burned to the ground. Whether they belonged to Ijaws or Itsekiris, she had no idea. It was people that lived in them. She thought of Tonye and guilt gripped through the core of her being. She avoided looking at Auntie Eyitemi because she knew the woman would read her mind in an instant.

She had lied to Tonye. Tomorrow she would not be in Benin waiting for him. Tomorrow she would be on the first flight to Lagos and in two weeks she would be back in England. She had made up her mind for them, even though he was yet not aware of that. She just could not stand the pressure any longer. She wished she had been strong enough to tell Tonye the truth. To tell him that she loved him with every fibre of her being, and that she loved him too much to stand by and watch them go through hell to marry her. She wished she had had the strength to look him in the eyes and told him to move on.

"Laju are you alright?" Auntie Eyitemi asked.

"I'm fine auntie," Laju said, still looking out the window and at the trees as they went by.

"Laju I know what you must be going through, but you have to be strong."

"I'm fine auntie," Laju said again and kept on counting the passing trees. She could not stop crying and she wondered if she ever would.

Fourteen.

Jolomi, Toritseju and Oyinmiebi

JOLOMI BEGAN TO TAKE PICTURES the moment he saw the warships as they approached. The village soon fell into utter chaos as people ran for their lives. He took pictures even as women screamed and gathered their children often tripping over the wide basin filled with rainwater they had gathered during the last rainfall. He took pictures even as the stronger men rushed into their small huts re-emerging with guns and cutlasses and as the weaker ones ran for hiding. He took pictures even as the warships drew closer and closer to the shores of the river. Someone ran past him and screamed something to him in Ijaw that he did not understand. Jolomi could feel his heart beat even faster. He was scared but he knew he had to face his fear and face the *boys* when they got off their boats.

Everything happened so fast. Time indeed stood still.

Jolomi heard a sound and the next thing he saw was a hut exploding. The force of the explosion was so strong that it threw Jolomi off his feet and onto the hard ground. He tasted blood in his mouth and he chewed on sand as he struggled to get up. His camera flew out of his hand. He looked around and rushed for it as soon as he saw it a few yards away from where he had landed. The village was empty when the attack started. Jolomi could not hear much at this point, but he knew for sure that an exchange of firepower had begun between the few village men with guns and the Itsekiri militia that was gaining ground. It was clear now, what he needed to do if he ever wanted to see Toritseju again; he had to hide. Jolomi had noticed that the thick mangrove forest was accessible from just a few yards away from him, so he picked himself up from the crouching position he had remained after grabbing his camera and began to make for the mangroves.

Everything happened much faster than he had expected. The first bullet came from nowhere and cut him on his leg. Jolomi screamed as he tripped and landed on his face. He heard his jaw break and pain ran errands all over his body. He grabbed his leg as blood gushed out. He looked up at the edge of the mangrove just a few yards away and he knew for sure now, that he had to get in there and hide; he turned to look at the shore of the river and saw that the boats had docked.

The attack was merciless. Men with bazookas stood from an angle and just pressed the trigger. Whatever was in the direction of the bazooka didn't stand a chance.

Jolomi began to crawl his way towards the mangrove trees. The closer he got to the edge of the mangroves the more he could hear shouts, and screams, and the explosions, and the gunshots.

At last, within the bamboo trees of the mangrove

168

forest, Jolomi grabbed one of the trees and supported himself as he tried to stand up. His leg hurt him so. Blood trickled from the corner of his mouth. Jolomi could see from where he stood within the dense bamboo populated forest, as the village went up in flames. He looked around him and then he saw the women, children and men cowering in fear everywhere within the forest. One of the men put his index finger on his lips and Jolomi nodded.

The next bullet ripped through Jolomi's chest. It had come without a warning, just like the first one. He screamed as he felt his chest explode. He fell on his side to the mushy earth and as he groaned in pain from the ground, he could see the rest of the people hiding, scatter further into the forest. They must have feared that his scream would attract the militia to their hiding place, but no one came. No one came to his rescue. The noise stopped now. Jolomi could not hear anything anymore. The gunshots had stopped and so had the explosions.

Jolomi did not know how for long he remained like that, bleeding out within the bamboo trees of the mangrove forest of Angbarama, going in and out of consciousness. Now he could hear the village come back to life. He could hear women scream as they discovered the dead bodies of their husbands and sons, of their daughters raped and mutilated beyond recognition.

Jolomi began to weep as he thought of his Toritseju. He wanted to go back home to her alive, to tell her he would never leave her side again. But he did not know if that was possible. He did not see help coming. He did not see himself in a fancy hospital bed in a fancy ward in

New York, with his Toju looking down at him with the most beautiful smile in the world on her face. So Jolomi did something any smart journalist in his situation would do. He managed to bring out his camcorder from his backpack as he felt himself become weaker and turned it on his face. If he didn't make it home alive, there was no way he was going out without telling Toritseju how much he loved her and how sorry he was for putting her through so much pain.

*

It'd been five days since Jolomi disappeared into the dusk of dawn from their home. Five days since Toritseju saw her neighborhood go up in flames. Five days of agony. Five days of pain. Five days of waiting, sick and dying with worry and without a word from Jolomi or his whereabouts. Toritseju could not take it any longer. She could not take the pain; the anxiety of sitting at home, amid fear, waiting for her husband to come home. She had cried her last drop of tear and she did not know what to do anymore. War had taken over the city of Warri and no one was safe even in one's own house. She wondered even now how she had managed to get the courage and strength to go back home after what she had experienced and seen five days ago. Her house had been, for some reasons unbeknownst to her, spared from burning down by warring youths. Around her lay a vast pile of rubble and debris. Fear was the order of the day. For her, it was fear and acute anxiety.

There hadn't been much fighting and destruction in the last two days, but Warri was like a graveyard with no one around but ghosts and shadows of what used to be.

Toritseju had reported Jolomi missing to the police the day after he didn't come back home at night, five days ago. Despite their hands filling with trying to keep peace and order in the city they had searched for him – or so they claimed – and there was still no sign of him. She had tried to contact Chief Warebi, whom Jolomi had spent too much time with at the detriment of his own good, but she heard the Chief's whereabouts were also unknown.

The kettle began to whistle in her small kitchen and she went to turn off the gas cooker. She lost her appetite for food. This was when she and Jolomi would settle for a nice plate of *eba* and *egusi soup* well prepared with *ugu* leaves and Tilapia fish. But now, she just couldn't find it in her to eat. Not while her husband was nowhere. Toritseju feared for the worst. They lived in terrible times. She thought back to Jolomi's days before she had met him; how radical a journalist he was and how far he would go to get the 'perfect' story. Nigeria did not produce enough of his type. She was so proud of him, but still she wished he wasn't so heroic. She wished he had been a 'normal' man who had gone to school to become a lawyer, or a doctor or a teacher. But then she wondered what their lives would be like now.

Toju slumped on a chair as the silence within her little house began to creep up on her. She felt its hands grope at her soft skin. She could hear it speak things to her that she did not want to condescend to. She could see its red eyes become even redder as it stared at her right in her eyes. She could feel the sharpness of its scale as it caressed her soft skin just before it raped her mind and ravaged her sanity. Was the silence a serpent? It was a beast sent from hell to torment her. She was going mad. She folded her legs onto the chair and hugged herself as she felt a sudden urge to scream. But the silence within their little apartment just wouldn't let her.

She wondered if their neighbors were still inside their own apartments too. Hiding!

Or they also were waiting for a loved one who had gotten up at four in the morning and had walked out into the dawn of a day that was so unpredictable. Or they had packed their bags and had fled to their little villages far away from the war, where peace wasn't such a luxury.

Toritseju prayed for at least some distraction.

Where were the noisy neighbor's hyperactive children when she needed them to cause some ruckus that would deliver her from the hands of such venomous silence?

Where were the kids from across the hallway that would come to her door and knock and then run away just as she answered the door?

Where was Angelica, her illiterate prostitute-turn-evangelist neighbor who would invite herself over and tell her the same old story of how *the Lord* had saved her soul one fateful day a thousand years ago while attending a Reinhard Bonnke crusade – which by the way she didn't want to attend in the first place because she had customers waiting.

Where was Alaere, one of her young and beautiful nurses from Warri General Hospital who would walk to her home and stay and chat with her while she cooked and waited for Jolomi to come back from one of his *fact-finding* missions? But again, she remembered that it was Alaere who had suggested to her that Jolomi was having an affair all those many times he was away, so she had stopped her from coming to her house all together.

Toritseju missed her family. She wished she could go home, but she was not going to leave the city without Jolomi, and she was not leaving her patients.

The silence was so deafening that Toritseju did not hear the heavy bangs on the door the first three times. When the banging got her attention, she jumped to her feet and rushed to the door.

It must be the police with news about Jolomi, she thought. She unlocked the door to see two young men standing outside.

"Good afternoon madam, please we are looking for Doctor Toju Benson," the first man said.

"I am Toju Benson. Is everything alright?" Toritseju froze the moment she asked the question.

That was when she saw it.

It was his.

She could recognize that backpack anywhere. He had been using it since his trip to Rwanda. But where was he? Where was her Jolomi?

"Where did you find this? Where is my husband?" Toritseju began to ask as she grabbed the bag from the young man's hand. She noticed how dirty the bag was.

She also noticed something too difficult to accept:

blood.

The man began to say something just when she began to swoon. She felt her head expand like a balloon blown too large and was about to pop. Sounds became muffled to her ears. She didn't hear what he was saying. She couldn't; she wasn't there anymore.

Earlier...

It was a brutal battle; the things that went on inside Oyinmiebi's head after watching Jolomi's last video entry on his camcorder for the seventh time. It'd been five days since 'black Monday' as the media had come to call that day. That fateful day when daylight turned into darkness and the sky in Warri blackened from the smoke and death-ash that ascended into the heavens. The same day that Oyinmiebi became a warrior to avenge the death of his Faith but ended up a messenger of love and sacrifice for a dying stranger who happened to be from the *enemy's* camp. The same day that Oyinmiebi had returned to Warri, glad to know his family was still alive, relinquished his gun, locked himself in his room, had a shower that he thought would never end and then wept like a baby for hours. That same day he had watched Jolomi's video and discovered who he was.

Zuokumo didn't give much thought to it after he had seen the videos. Neither did he lose sleep over the pictures on the journalist's digital camera. Those were things he had seen in real life and even taken part in. Nothing was new to him. But Oyinmiebi was torn up within himself by the conflict of whether to go out into the war-ridden city and look for Jolomi's wife and then be the one to give her the memorabilia of her husband's brutal death.

"You must do what is right by you, my son," his father had said when Oyinmiebi had told him all that had happened.

So, on this day, five days after black Monday, Oyinmiebi called Zuokumo and persuaded him to go with him into town and look for Jolomi's widow.

Warri was a desolate waste land when the cousins set out to find Jolomi's wife, Doctor Toju Benson. There was no one around. Marketplaces had either burned down or sat abandoned for fear of another round of violent attacks. Stores closed. Businesses had packed up and left the city. The heavy rains of March seemed to have done more harm than good. It seemed the city had washed away. Warri was not what it used to be. Rumour had it that the Federal Government was planning on declaring a State of Emergency on the city and deploy federal troops upon the city, but no one had seen any gun-slinging soldier yet and they were not ready to be caught with their pants down if or when the boys came. Everyone stayed indoors. And those who had the guts to move around, like Oyinmiebi and Zuokumo, did so with utmost caution.

Oyinmiebi could not make sense of how a city once filled with so much life could end up like this. He looked beside him at Zuokumo walking, a shadow of his former self. His hands swung by his sides. He wondered what went on in his mind. Zuokumo had seen so much during this time of violence. And since black Monday, he had withdrawn into himself. He spoke less and did too many chores within the house. Since the destruction of their house at Ogbe-Ijoh, Zuokumo had been living with Oyinmiebi and his family while Zuokumo's family remained in hiding safely in Ughelli.

Finding Jolomi's apartment wasn't as hard as they thought. It was quite a popular area, with lots of run-down living establishments and Oyinmiebi wondered how journalists like Jolomi with a wife who was a medical doctor, lived in a place like that. Well, there must be a story behind it.

It was Zuokumo's idea to bang on the door after Oyinmiebi had knocked twice and still no answer. They were about to turn around and leave when they heard the shuffle of feet from within the house. They stopped as the door opened.

"Good afternoon madam, we are looking for Doctor Toju Benson," Oyinmiebi said as he noticed how beautiful she was. She was more beautiful than she looked in the picture he had seen in the journalist's wallet.

Oyinmiebi felt his head swell to a point of explosion. Was he going to be the one to tell this young woman that her husband was dead; that he had died in the muddy trenches of the Angbarama bamboo mangrove forests?

"I am Doctor Benson. Is everything alright?" She asked. She had a soft voice.

Oyinmiebi had the journalist's backpack held in front of him and he could see from the sudden look on her face that she could recognize it. He could see her face turn pale in an instance. She grabbed her bosom as the tears that gathered in her eyes glistened like diamond dust.

"Where did you find this? Where is my husband?" She asked as she grabbed the bag from Oyinmiebi's hand.

"I'm sorry madam but your husband...oh my God Zuokumo, hold her."

The boys were not fast enough. The woman hit the ground within seconds. Oyinmiebi rushed to her side. He could see that she was still breathing.

"Zuokumo, look after her, let me get some water," Oyinmiebi said, calling to his cousin, who still stood outside the door, unflinching.

"Oyinmiebi, are you mad? Is it not enough that we brought her dead husband's things back to her? You want to nurse her or what?" Zuokumo asked, not moving from where he stood.

"What! How could you be so indifferent about this?" Oyinmiebi said. He was shocked when Zuokumo turned around and walked away, leaving him alone with the woman.

Oyinmiebi was determined to see this through. He was determined to make sure she was alright after she received the news that her husband died. He couldn't just leave her there. What if she did something to herself after she watched her husband's video log? Oyinmiebi found the kitchen, got some water, and began to nurse the journalist's wife back to life. He thought of the irony of the situation.

Hours later, after Toritseju had regained consciousness, Oyinmiebi told her that her husband was dead. He stayed there to catch her as she broke down in tears. He sat with her as she watched Jolomi's video message. He consoled her as she cried her eyes out even more. He held her as she began to shiver in pains and agony that Oyinmiebi could only imagine. He was with her all the way, that was all that mattered to him. That was his redemption. That was the beginning of his journey back to life.

Oyinmiebi was still with Toritseju when the news came that the Federal Government had declared a state of emergency in Warri and deployed Federal troops to impose law and order. When he stood up to leave, she already had neighbors and a few friends with her. He made her promise him that she would take care of herself and she made him promise to visit her and make sure she was alright. They both agreed.

Oyinmiebi walked a long while away from Toritseju's house before he broke down and let his tears start flowing. At last, he felt he could taste a slice of hope.

AFTERMATH.

A slice of hope... or not.

Dear Diary,

May 1997.

THEY CAME LIKE WILDFIRE *spreading through the dead city. They came like a terrible flood sent from the heavens to wash away the pains, sufferings, violence, destruction, and death that had gone on for too long. They came like a heavy gush of strong monsoon wind blowing away the piles of ashes of the dead souls that had been mounting up and reaching to the footstools of the gods. They came just when the people needed them, after having suffered the terrible war for three long months that never seemed to end. But they didn't come the way the people had envisaged. They didn't come as knights in shiny armours - to the rescue. They didn't come for damsels in distress. They didn't come for victims trapped in the trenches of war or in the unbreakable embrace of their own despair.*

Instead they came in armored tanks, with machine guns slung over their shoulders. They came with hearts made of metal. They came without warning. No one in Warri knew the day they would come, so there was no time to pack. There was no time at all!

They came as if they were on a mission to fight yet another battle and Warri was the ready battlefield.

So, in May of 1997 peace visited Warri but she came at a terrible price. She came with a dusk-till-dawn curfew. She came with whips and iron fists. She came with despoiling sons who were ready to bed all the daughters of Warri and fill their wombs with bastards who would grow up and never know their fathers.

And so, she came!

Peace!

But was the slice of hope that she served sweet, or filled with bitterness that you could only taste after you had chewed and swallowed?

My children got their way. I was leaving Warri in pieces - a battered and shattered woman. My heart broke. I was the shadow of myself. I had lost my friends. I had lost every hope I had. My children may have sent the driver to drive me to Ibadan, but I was leaving. I pray for Warri. I pray for her children.

This is my last diary entry in this diary. I am leaving to start a new life, and I do not want to remember and relive the event of the past three months, so I am letting go.

Goodbye Warri.

Fifteen.
May 2003.

THE SILENCE THAT DROWNED the
congregation was deep. No one said anything. Someone
might have offered applause, but given that it was a
funeral, there just wasn't any need for it. The young man
closed the diary from which he had been reading and
cleared his throat as he wiped the tears from his eyes. He
looked across to his sisters sitting with their husbands
and children on the front phew just a few yards away
from the casket and one of them nodded in approval. He
returned the nod and continued to speak.

"That was the last entry from our late mother's diary,"
Senator Matthew Ogheneovo concluded, with tears
rolling down his face. He paused again, as he allowed
himself some time to get himself together. He brought
out a handkerchief and wiped his tears before they got
any further down his face.

"A lot of you knew mama and how strong she was.
She was the best mother any one of us could ask for."
He thought of saying more but he thought it would be

wise not to, after reading from the diary. And besides his sisters had already given good eulogies. He adjusted his white flowing *agbada* as he stepped off the podium and began to walk to his mother's open casket.

She looked peaceful. He placed her diary on her chest and bent over to kiss her on her cold and dead cheek. He could hear the congregation gasp, but he didn't give it a thought.

The funeral was short but very well attended. Of course, everyone wanted to pay their respects to the man who may very well be the next Governor of Delta State. Although he had lost the gubernatorial race to the incumbent administration, the race was a close call. And it was obvious that the young senator was ambitious and had his eye set on higher grounds.

Two days after the funeral ended and most of the guests had travelled back, Tonye sat and waited for five hours to see the Senator in his country home. The large waiting room was filled with people who either wanted to pay some more tributes to the popular senator and those who just wanted to beg a favour or another from him. Tonye didn't mind the buzz that went around him. He didn't worry about the fact that he was subjecting himself, being the Senator's Chief of Staff, to waiting like that to see his boss and old colleague when he could just walk right through the private entrance and into the senator's private quarters. He just wanted to sit there for a while. He didn't mind that the man standing next to him had a body odour that set his stomach cringing. All that occupied his mind was what had happened the previous day. It had happened right out of the blue. It had happened like it was a scene from a Hollywood movie with a sick suspenseful twist to it that always led to happy conclusions.

Tonye had just finished one of his intense arguments with the senator. He was trying to convince the senator to contest the results of the just concluded elections and take the incumbent governor to an electoral tribunal but the senator in his usual tardiness had laughed and waved it aside.

"Come on Tonye, the elections were not rigged like you say they were," Senator Matthew said.

"Matthew, we are alone in this room. Please drop the unusual loyalty you have for this administration. You and I know the elections lied. Ballot boxes were stolen."

"Don't speak to me like that Tonye, I'm still a senator of the Federal Republic of Nigeria and your boss no less," Senator Matthew was trying hard to hold his growing irritation. Something with the way he sounded made him seem even unsure to himself, whether he was indeed who he said he was.

"Spare me that talk Matthew. We've been friends for how long now, about twenty years?" Tonye said. The senator remained silent. He didn't investigate the angry face of his beloved friend.

"If your loyalty wasn't so unfounded, you would not have picked the ticket to run against him in the first place knowing how it would end."

"Tonye you don't understand."

"Oh, I do. I just didn't believe that any of the rumours

were true. I guess I was wrong."

Both men remained silent for a minute, each facing an opposite direction. Tonye stood up and walked up to the built-in mini-bar and poured himself a drink from a bottle of Jack Daniel's Tennessee Whiskey.

"Do you want some, Senator?" He asked. The sarcasm was like a sharp double-edged sword in his voice. The senator turned and opened his mouth to protest but thought against it. "Yes please," he said instead.

Tonye poured the senator a drink and took it to him. He waited for him to start drinking before he began to speak again.

"I'm leaving Matthew," Tonye said and sipped his Hennessey waiting for Matthew to react. Matthew remained silent.

"Did you hear what I said? I put in my resignation and a list of recommended people who could take my place. I want to go back to England, Matthew. I'm tired of *all* this," Tonye added, using his hands more than he was using his voice as he spoke.

"I didn't think you saw her yesterday Tonye," Matthew said and turned to face his friend who looked a little too clueless about what he was talking.

Tonye finished his drink and walked to the chair next to his friend.

"Saw *who* Matthew? What are you talking about? Did you even hear what I said? I said I quit."

"Laju," Matthew said and this time he had Tonye's full attention.

"I beg your pardon."

"Laju, Tonye."

"You saw *Laju* yesterday? Where? When? How?" Tonye said jumping to his feet and taking a step away from Matthew. It was as if he had just found out that the good senator was a leper.

"Sit down Tonye. You mean you didn't know that she was around this whole time?"

"No, I did not. Where is she? I mean, do you know *where* she is?"

"Tonye, what are you going to do? She is married now. With two children as I heard. Turns out her husband is one of my highest supporters and donors."

Tonye was silent.

"Married with children. Wow! That's interesting," Tonye said and began to laugh. Matthew looked at him, wondering if his friend had gone mad.

"Tonye, is everything alright?"

"Matthew, this woman almost ruined my life, and she is the reason why I am still single after she drove off right in front of me never to be seen or heard from again for six years and here, she reappears, married with children. I'm impressed. Let me guess, he is Itsekiri, right?" Tonye said as tears welled up in his eyes. He didn't know why the tears had appeared. He thought he had gotten over his heartbreak a long time ago. He wondered why the talk of Laju still brought tears to his eyes.

"What does it matter what tribe he is from? She has moved on and so should you."

"Then do me just one favour, Matthew, as your most trusted friend. Let me go. Accept my resignation, give me a severance, and let me go back to England and pursue a life there. I have held on to her for six years."

"I want to, Tonye. But you must know, that it is hard for me to just accept your resignation and watch you go after all you have put in to my political career and office."

"You will find someone better, trust me."

"You think so? Can anyone be a better bulldozer than you?"

"I will make sure you get the best replacement for me."

"Oh Tonye, I cannot believe it has come to this. That you would resign because I refused to take a piece of your advice," Matthew said.

"Matthew, you know it's not about that."

"Then what is this talk of resignation all about?"

Tonye heaved a heavy sigh.

"Matthew you will not understand. All the things you read from your mother's diary were things *I* experienced first-hand. You were still in the UK when Warri went dark in 1997. After Laju left, and I followed on her heels but never found her, I came back to Warri and I have lived my life since then trying to forget all the things I saw in the two weeks I stayed, before I fled. It took me a lot of courage to return to help you with your politics in

2000. Now that Laju has resurfaced, I want to leave more than ever before."

"Tonye, I may not have been here in 1997, but the war is far from over. Now it is the turn of the Urhobos and Itsekiris. It's crazy."

"Well, I read the papers and I follow the news even though, thank God, we are in Abuja. I know what's been going on, but I just don't want to be a part of it anymore. I am tired of fighting unnecessary battles that were never meant to be fought in the first place."

Matthew cleared his throat before he spoke.

"I see. I accept your resignation and I promise you will get your severance whenever you are ready to leave," Matthew said.

"Thank you, Senator."

"Oh, spare me the 'senator' crap. You already trashed me enough for one day. Now would you like to know how to find Laju or not?" Matthew asked.

Tonye had not expected his friend to say that, but again, his friend could see right through him. It was obvious he was itching to know.

"Well, I don't know what I should do when I see her."

"You need to see her Tonye. Close the chapter and move on, for the last time. God brought her here for this. I didn't even know who might attend mama's funeral. You out-sourced the PR and none of us knew. I mean, how could I not have known she was married to one of my supporters?" Matthew said.

"Yeah, beats me. Or perhaps, you knew I would have been even more disoriented if I had known from the moment you knew so you chose to spare me the agony."

"Or that," Matthew said and laughed.

Tonye turned from the open window he was looking out from to look at his fattened friend, as his laughter shook the very floor on which they stood.

"Did you know?" Tonye asked as he realized that he may have been playing to Matthew's tunes for a while.

"I only knew since a few months ago. I swear I would have told you, but I was busy with the paperwork involved in bringing back Mama's body from the US."

"Matthew, *I* was busy with the said paperwork. And *I* was also busy trying to get you to win an election."

"There you have it. I didn't want that kind of distraction on your shoulders."

Tonye scowled at his friend as if he would strangle him.

"Please Matthew, do you know where she might be?" Tonye asked trying to sound as calm as possible.

"I will get the driver to take you there. Take it easy Tonye. Laju is married to a powerful man."

Tonye scoffed.

"What do you think I want to do? Kidnap her and force her to marry me?" He laughed and wondered if he even had the slightest feeling of love left in him for Laju.

The driver took him straight to the house he recognized ever so well. Grandmother Dawson's mansion. It was just as he had last seen it. It had been repainted but with the same snaring colour that said, 'AN OLD HAG LIVES HERE. YOU WILL BE SHOT DEAD IF YOU TRESPASS'.

Tonye's heart wouldn't stop pounding. He just remained, unmoved, in the back of the tinted government car. He sat there frozen, as the sight of the house brought back so many bad memories. He was about to ask the driver to take him back to Matthew's house when the grandiose door swung open and Laju, looking the same as she had the last time he saw, her six years ago. His heart stopped dead on its tracks. He knew there and then that he never stopped loving her. He could not move as he watched her rush to a car whose door stood open thanks to a uniform chauffeur. Just then a child rushed out of the house and ran after her, screaming and crying, waving her hands in the air until Laju turned and crouched to grab the crying child in the motherliest embrace Tonye had ever seen.

His heart started beating again. He just didn't think anymore. He opened the door and moved out of the car in one swift move. As he slammed the car door behind him, Laju turned. He had a smile on his face as he stood there across the road and waved at her as he noticed how frozen to death she was.

He began to cross the road over to the Dawson mansion as she began to walk towards the gate, her daughter trailing behind her.

The short walk across the road seemed like it would never end. Tonye thought of the best words with which he could start talking to Laju, but no words seemed to be coming to his head.

He saw her for the first time, as he reached the gate which was the only thing that separated him from Laju now. The girl was hiding behind her mother, spying, and smiling and making funny faces at the stranger who seemed to be staring at her peculiarly. Tonye knew that smile. He knew that perfect set of dentitions. He knew that face; that very funny face. The face of *his* mother, he could recognize it, even replicated as the face of a child. Tears welled up in his eyes before he could find a way to conceal them. Rather than speaking to Laju, who was herself too shocked to say anything, he went on one knee and spoke instead to the little girl.

"How old are you darling?" Tonye asked.

"Hi. I am six. How old are you?" The little girl replied and Tonye grabbed his heart as he felt it break into a million pieces.

"Oh my God, Laju. You could do *this* to me," he said. He found it hard to get up again.

"Tonye…" Laju began but her voice trailed away as Tonye stared into the eyes of this little angel who was no doubt *his* flesh and bone. What lies had Laju fed her yet? Did she know that she called a stranger 'daddy'? Did she know that *this* strange stranger was her father?

Tonye felt Laju's hand helping him to his feet. He had not known when she had opened the gate and come to his side. He stood up and followed her as she led him into Grandmother Dawson's mansion, into her Persian living room. He did not remove his shoes before he entered, and he wondered since when had Grandmother

Dawson begun to compromise the rug in her living room.

The little girl never left his side as she must've wondered what was wrong with him.

Tonye saw a glass of water, which he accepted and gulped down at once.

"I tried to tell you, but by then I was too far gone, and I could not contact you," Laju offered to explain, but Tonye could hear her voice stream right into his left ear and escape from the right one.

"What did you name her?" He asked instead.

"Oritsemuyiwa Alexandra Ferguson," Laju said.

"Ferguson."

"That's my husband's name. He knows everything."

"I want her back," Tonye said.

Laju didn't fight back.

"I want to be a part of her life. She must know the truth. And you must start by naming her Tamaralayefa Kemefa. She can keep the Itsekiri and other names, but she is not a Ferguson. She is mine. Ours. Yours and mine," he said, still avoiding looking at Laju's face. He knew she had been crying from the moment she had helped him get back up on his feet outside the Dawson mansion.

"I swear I didn't mean to hurt you Tonye. I loved you with all my heart," she said.

He turned to look at her for the first time and Tonye saw that age had not been so kind to her. He could see six years written all over her face. He knew she had six years of experience that she could tell him about, but he didn't want to know about it.

"I loved you too, Laju. I was ready to beat them all, for you," he said.

"I know. I didn't want you to. It would have been too much pain and suffering," Laju added. Just then her maid walked in, leading a little boy of about four years old in. He had just woken up from sleep. He rushed into Laju's bosom and she began to rub his back.

"This here is Ayomide Louis Ferguson Junior," Laju said, managing a smile.

Tonye smiled at the little boy and he could see the striking resemblance he bore to his powerful oil magnate father.

"Laju, I'm sorry life dealt us bad cards," Tonye said and stood up. Laju sprung up after him. Her eyes told him that there was still so much she wished she could say, but Tonye didn't want to hear her story. Not now. He had come to close a chapter and move on with his life. But he had opened a whole new world for him and although he had Laju to thank for keeping their daughter, he didn't think he owed her any gratitude.

"I will draw up the legal papers and come back tomorrow, Laju. Get a lawyer. Nothing serious, just that I am Tamaralayefa's father and that I will be a part of her life forever." He went on one knee again and smiled at the little girl who for some reason lit up whenever he went close to her.

He began to leave when Laju grabbed his sleeve and

fell on her knees.

"I am sorry Tonye. These words have haunted me for the past six years and the only thing that kept me sane was looking at our daughter's face and how much she looked like you and knowing that I still had a part of you."

Tonye looked at her and extended his hand to her. He pulled her up and pulled her to a tight embrace.

"I forgive you," he whispered into her ear before he let her go and turned to leave; a happy man.

*

"Tonye, why did you have to wait here with all these people?" A familiar voice said as a hand shook him from his slumber. He looked up into the face of the senator's wife who also was a dear friend of his.

Tonye stood up and allowed her to lead him into the kitchen.

"Matthew is engaged in some stupid meeting. The maid told me you were sleeping in there. Jesus, are you alright? You look awful. Have you eaten? I must make you some tea first," the woman went on. Tonye wondered who talked more, the husband or the wife.

"Esther, you will not believe what news I have," Tonye said with a smile reaching from each end of his face as a hot pot of tea brewed just for him.

Sixteen.
May 2003.

MOGHA'S LEFT ARM HUNG by his side as he ran through the busy and overcrowded corridors of the Lagos University Teaching Hospital where he was doing his residency. He ran through the endless queues of patients waiting to consult with a physician, past the awful but harmless stench of the general toilets drowned with gallons of acidic antiseptics, past the nurses' station with all the young and beautiful but stuck-up nurses with their noses always up in the air. Mogha was running late for his Advanced Anatomy class as usual. It'd been going on like that since the semester had started, after his sudden transfer from the University of Benin where he had started out in. He knew he had to step up if he intended to graduate with honours – or at all for that matter – by the end of the year. But that day he had ample reason for being so late.

It was 5:30am when his cell phone had rung. He knew who it was. He had been expecting that call for a few days. With his eyes still held captive by sleep, he had picked up the phone and the moment he had heard his father's voice, sleep had let him go.

At last, they were coming back home. Their ticket reservations made, and suitcases parked, their minds made up: they were coming back home to Nigeria.

After their experience in Warri six years ago, Mogha and Seye had returned to the UK. Mogha had gone through a series of physiotherapy sessions due to the limpness of his left arm and after everything; he had accepted his arm like that since it functioned just as well as his right. He had the choice to stay back in the UK and go to school there, a choice that Seye had jumped at with open arms, but Mogha had returned. He had gone back to school, repeated an entire year and after finding his feet in school and making it to his final year; he had decided to do his residency in the Lagos University Teaching Hospital without once leaving Nigeria.

Mogha was so excited to have his brother back. Seye had never come back to Nigeria until now.

It had been six years. Six long years had gone by – no less than a whirlwind for the brothers– since they fled their home in Warri. Six agonizing years it had been for the Aroromi's during which time they had gone through the long and excruciating journey of recovering their sanity and happiness.

Mogha ran into a patient.

"Sorry" he said over his shoulder, as he raced to meet up with his classmates, but nonetheless, he still found his mind wandering.

"Glad you could join us my young man," Professor R.

E Stone said in her usual shaky voice as Mogha snuck into the lecture room. Nothing went past the near-70-year-old German Professor. Everyone, including national and international Medical Journals regarded her as a genius in the field of Anatomy and Medicine but her students just knew her as 'the Cadaver Goddess" – behind her back, of course.

"I'm sorry ma'am," Mogha offered.

"Oh, come now, join in," she said waving for him to join the near-empty amphitheater-style lecture room. Mogha wondered where all the other students were. They were tired of seeing deceased bodies – the professor always taught with those.

Mogha joined his classmates around the gurney on which was a female cadaver cut open from the neck to the belly-button. Mogha was unmoved. He had seen worse.

"As I was saying, today we will determine the cause of death of this person lying here before you," Professor Stone continued, but with every word she said, Mogha found himself being pulled away from where he was, back into a past he had tried hard to bury deep within himself for the past six years.

*

"Well, you are a lucky young man, Mogha. Good thing your brother brought you here when he did yesterday. It could've have been a different story by now," Doctor Toju said with a warm smile, the day after the bullet was retrieved from Mogha's shattered left shoulder. He had just regained consciousness from the anesthesia administered to him before the doctors began to work on him. His head still felt a little fuzzy. But worst of all, he couldn't feel his left arm at all. He reached and grabbed it with his right hand, a gesture to make sure that his arm still hung there.

"Don't worry my dear; your arm is still intact. We didn't need to take it from you," the beautiful doctor said with a smile. "But you may feel some numbness for a while; it's from the morphine we had to administer directly into the arm in case you woke up in pain. It will pass."

"Oh, thank God. I was so scared."

"You don't have to be."

"Thank you, Doctor. I am indeed lucky to have a brother like Seye," Mogha said. His throat ached as he spoke.

"Glad to hear that. I must get a move on now. As you know, things are crazy out there and we have tons of patients to take care of. I will check on you later. In the meantime, have you sent a word to your parents to get you?" Toritseju asked. Her question went to Seye, who had remained silent all this time.

"No ma, no one knows where we are at the moment." Seye said.

"I don't understand."

"We had just arrived in from the UK when we were ambushed in our home. Our father didn't know we were coming so he had fled before we got there."

"Oh my God! This is terrible. I am so sorry. I mean,

we all have had our fair share of tragedy in the past few days but this…" Her voice trailed off as if trying to hold herself from weeping.

"But we know where our father is. He's in Benin City and we are supposed to be on our way there now, to meet him," Seye added.

"Oh. But you cannot go. It's not safe out there. We are lucky to have security forces guiding the hospital; I cannot say the same for the city. And besides Mogha still needs some time to recover."

"But doctor…." Seye began to protest but stopped when he felt Mogha's good hand on his shoulder.

"How long will it take me to recover?" Mogha asked looking at the doctor.

"At least a few days. It's too soon to tell. It may be less depending on how things turn out. It's just not safe for anyone right now."

"Okay doctor. Thank you," Mogha said and he saw how much Seye wanted to protest but he was glad his brother had said noting.

"What was that? You know we have to be on our way to find dad," Seye protested after the doctor had left.

"I know, Seye."

"Then why did you let the doctor convince us to stay? I don't want to stay here Mogha. I'm scared out of my pants. Not after what we went through yesterday."

"I'm scared too, Seye and I do not want to be here anymore than you do."

"Then we have to get out of here. I have not slept since yesterday. I had nightmares even with my eyes wide open. I stared at you all through the night, watching you breathe, praying that your chest shouldn't stop heaving up and down."

"I know Seye. But we must be careful indeed," Mogha said. He was sure Seye could hear the weakness in his voice. He just hoped his younger brother would understand.

"What do we do now?" Seye asked, a little calmer.

"We wait for a while."

"How long Mogha? Jesus! Do you have any idea what Dad may be going through right now? He must have confirmed by now from Serena, that we left the UK for Nigeria and remember we didn't go to Auntie's house in Lagos, so they haven't seen us either. Please think about him too," Seye said.

Mogha saw tears sparkle in his eyes but Seye did not cry.

Mogha was silent for a while, buried deep in his own confusion.

"Seye, what do you want us to do?" Mogha said. Seye heaved a heavy sigh of relief.

"Good. As soon as it gets dark and the hospital is less crowded, we make a run for it."

"Is that your plan?"

"What else did you think I had in mind? Call for a cab?" Seye retorted and Mogha shut up. He was impressed at how much stronger his brother had become, all in one day.

"And then what?"

"Mogha, Benin City is not far from here. Once we get a taxi and tell him we will pay him whatever his price is, he would take us."

"Ok. I want to get out of here, just so you know."

"I know bro."

Mogha was sleeping when he felt his brother shake him out of slumber. He knew it was time. He looked around, it was dark everywhere, except for the few corridor lights and a few other fluorescent tubes flickering at various places in the hospital. Two other patients came in earlier to join the brothers, but they were asleep or unconscious on their beds. Both had severe burn wounds all over their bodies and Mogha wondered how they had survived such excruciating injuries. He could hear their heavy and painful breathing. He could see their chests wrapped in bandages heave up and down. They looked like fresh, mummified Egyptian kings but without any sign of the royalty and splendor that went into the burial of an Egyptian with royal blood.

The smell in the ward was different from earlier before.

It was stronger.

Worse!

It smelled of dead and cooked meat, and Mogha realized how hungry he was. He hated himself for feeling hungry at the smell of burnt human flesh. He watched as Seye tiptoed, the briefcase in one hand, to the door and opened it.

Within minutes they were out of the ward and making their way through the corridors to the nurses' station just a few steps away from the main entrance door. The hospital corridors filled with people – patients no doubt – sleeping on the bare floor. Most of them wore blood like splattered paint. Some had bloody bandages around various parts of their body.

Mogha didn't feel so good. He felt his stomach cringe. Was it from the hunger? He wondered. Or was he just nauseated by what he was seeing? He wondered how Seye could be so strong and unflinching.

Mogha felt odd. It was then he realized that he still could not feel his left arm. He grabbed it with his good right hand and pinched himself so hard that he thought his skin would peel right off but still he did not feel anything. He began to panic but he didn't say anything. He didn't tell Seye what was wrong. He didn't want to cause more panic than they were already in. He just held on to his paralyzed arm and continued behind Seye, as they both found their footing amidst the sea of bodies lying on the ground and made their way out.

At the nurses' station two nurses were engaged in a whispery discussion. Clapping their hands silent – they just had to clap. Throwing and waving their hands in the air – maybe they chased the mosquitoes that seemed like warriors themselves these days.

Before the boys could make another move, the nurses spotted them and stopped whispering.

"Where are you two going?" One of the nurses asked.

She was so thin that Mogha thought he saw her head wobble as she spoke.

"Good evening madam. We are leaving," Seye said and before Mogha could say what he wasn't ready to say.

"Ah, so late? Why don't you wait until tomorrow?" The second, much fatter nurse said.

"We cannot. The hospital is getting fuller by the minute, and we need to be on our way to Benin City right now," Seye said and grabbed Mogha by his bad arm and pulled him as he began to make his way towards the main exit. Mogha cried out in pain.

"Oh my God. I'm sorry. Are you alright?" Seye stopped and asked letting go of his brother. The nurses leaned forward to watch the drama that was unfolding before them, but they didn't move, nor did they try to stop them from leaving.

"I'm fine. I'm fine. I couldn't feel my arm before, now I feel pain and it feels good," Mogha said and he knew everyone must think he was going insane.

"Let's go bro," Seye said and helped his brother as they walked out of Warri General Hospital.

They breathed fresh air and it felt good even though the air filled with the ashes of the innocent casualties of this unnecessary war.

It was pitch-black outside, but the boys took one step forward, and then one after another, they began their long walk towards freedom and salvation.

Many years later, the boys would still tell this story. The story of their quest for survival in a land they once called home but became too afraid to even visit after 1997; of all that they had experienced that fateful day when they had decided to surprise their beloved father by showing up without calling first. They would tell the story of how they had walked for about four hours the night they left the Warri General Hospital until they had begun to see the signs of the breaking of a new day, before they saw the first taxi and how after three more taxis, one taxi driver agreed to drive them to Benin City if they paid him whatever he demanded. Mogha would tell the story of how his left arm came to hang beside him but was still just as strong as his right arm; he would recount the story over and over to his patients. Just before he administered his syringe, he would explain how he had feared he was becoming paralyzed, and how pain took away his paralysis.

*

"Class dismissed," Professor R. E. Stone said and Mogha jolted back to reality. The *cadaver goddess* was staring right at him from across the gurney.

"My young man, I need a one-page essay on what I taught today on my desk first thing tomorrow. For now, I will overlook your utter sense of distraction in my class, but next time I will not be so merciful," she said looking at him from above her gold-rimmed glasses.

"Yes professor. I'm sorry ma, please…"

"*Gib mir eine pause. Nur raus,*" she muttered under her breath in a thick German accent. Mogha jumped to his feet. "Essay. First thing tomorrow. Go," she said pointing to the door as other students scrambled out for their next class.

Seventeen.
May 2003.

"JOLOMI PLEASE STOP playing with those," Toritseju said to her six-year-old son as he knocked down the award statuettes and glass figurines which had been arranged on a decorating mantle. Toritseju stood up from the show she was watching on the television and went over to her son.

"My God, you are growing so fast. I have to look for somewhere higher to keep these," she mumbled as she took the protesting child by the hand and led him away. As soon as his attention was elsewhere, she went back to the mantle and began to rearrange. It was a routine to which she must have adjusted for a while now.

Toritseju picked up one of the statuettes and looked down at it. The inscription on the square-shaped base on which the statuette stood read, "*CNN International Journalist of the Year 1994*". She smiled and replaced it on the same spot where it always was. It brought back memories; great memories and bad ones too.

"Mummy, when is grandma coming back?" Little

Jolomi asked from across the living room.

Toritseju could hear the signature sound of *Tom & Jerry* and she knew her son had changed the channel. That, of all his many sources for pranks, was where he got most of his pranks from. Toritseju sighed and went back to join her son.

"Well, grandma said she would be back in a jiffy, didn't she?"

"Well, that is always what she says every time she visits us, and she never comes back again until after one year," the boy said looking up at his mother.

"One year? Jolomi, you mean one week. Grandma comes here every weekend to play with you. Now she had to go and take care of grandpa for a *weetle* while."

"Mummy, I'm not a kid anymore. It's 'little' not *weetle*."

"Oh, I see, someone is a big boy now. Come here you," she teased and went to tickle him. The little boy screamed in laughter as he tried to break free from his mother.

Moments later, while in the kitchen as Jolomi napped on the sofa, Toritseju recounted the two significant phone calls she had had within the last three days. A smile lingered on her face as the words of the stranger with the British accent came back to her.

"Doctor Benson, I am glad to inform you that after much consideration and after seeing the response your husband's final news piece drew from around the world, the United Nations and the BBC are conferring a posthumous award for his selfless service in good journalism."

She had remained silent while the female caller had continued talking about her pre-arranged flight and hotel reservations, about someone who was already in place to pick them up from Heathrow Airport and drop them off at their hotel. The woman gave her every detail and somehow Toju took it all in; all that time slumped into a chair, holding the phone to her ears as she let the tears pour out from her eyes.

Her mother had been visiting then. When she had told her the news, both women had cried in sheer joy.

And then the next day after that call, the *Doctors Without Borders* department attached to the United Nations had called to congratulate her on her husband's award –the word had gone around – and to offer her a job as a medical adviser and consultant with the UN. It was more than she had hoped for.

After Jolomi's death, Toritseju had thought she had lost every reason to live. But two days after she got the news of Jolomi's death while a colleague came to pay her condolences, the woman had taken one look at her and had said, "Toju are you pregnant?"

She had done a test, and as soon as she confirmed that she was indeed pregnant, it restored her will. And that had made all the difference.

She didn't stay in Warri long enough after that to see the city fall to the ground. She wasn't there when the military took over, all that she heard about much later. She had just parked wherever she could and had boarded the next bus out of the city. During her last days in Warri she had tried everything she could to recover Jolomi's body, but they never did find Jolomi's body. The funeral was well-attended in Lagos. It was a closed-casket ceremony and it was too painful for her to bear.

There were days after that, during her months of pregnancy while living with her parents, when she would think she could hear him call her name. She would walk, as if in a trance, to the window and look out for any sign of Jolomi returning home and when she wouldn't see anything she would scream on the top of her lungs until her mother, father, brother or all three would rush to her side. Sometimes she would feel him lying right beside her and she would jump up - and then he would be gone.

It was a terrible time for Toritseju, those eight and half months, mourning the death of her husband and going through pregnancy without him. Her parents and younger brother had been her foundation and strength.

After Little Jolomi arrived, he had brought with him the light she had needed to find her way back to liberation. He had come as a split-image of his father. That was when Toritseju knew that she had work yet to do.

Three months after the birth of her son, Toritseju fished out Jolomi's camera and this time while breast-feeding their son, watched it repeatedly and cried her eyes out until she had a headache. After that, she had made duplicate copies and had sent each with a passionate letter she had written, to all the news stations she could think about.

The NTA was the first to air it and it became a smashing new eye-opener into the Warri incident of

1997. CNN aired it during a documentary on the Warri Crisis and by then Little Jolomi was already on all fours crawling all around every corner of the house. The awards began to pour in and so did the criticism.

After she went public with her decision to start the *Jolomi Benson Foundation and Center for Grief Counselling and Rehabilitation,* a lot of people accused her of capitalizing on the death of her husband to pursue fame and fortune. So, one day after thinking long and hard enough, she agreed to an interview with a syndicated talk show host and after the whole country watched and heard her recount what she went through after Jolomi's death and why she had to release the footages, she caught a break. Her reasons had been simple: Jolomi's body disappeared out there, and so should his message.

Jolomi's News - as most international news networks came to call it did bring in a lot of money for her, but she still hadn't spent anything from it. She was saving it for Little Jolomi's college fund, she had told her mother one day. And all the donations she got from her work at the center went into charity and helping people.

"Mummy I'm hungry," little Jolomi's voice jolted her.

"Oh, my baby, when did you wake up?" she asked going to him.

"Just now. I want crackers."

"Ok. Crackers it is. What do you say; let me make you some nice pasta after crackers?"

"Hmm... I don't know. I'll have to think about it," the little boy said laughing.

"You are such a funny little man Jolomi," Toritseju said as she stretched to reach the box of crackers high up in the kitchen cabinet. She wondered why she had to keep it in such a difficult place to reach.

As she watched her son eat, Toritseju wondered when it would be the right time to tell her son about his father. He had come home from school asking about him so many times and every time she had averted the question, now she thought he had given up on trying to know.

"Mummy, Morenike has a daddy. Why don't I have one?" he had asked on one of those days after school. The question had thrown her off her feet and she had almost dropped the glass of water from which she was drinking.

But as usual she had found a way to change the topic. She didn't think he was ready for it yet.

Three weeks later, while Toritseju and little Jolomi sat teasing each other at the departure lounge of the Lagos International Airport, a man walked up to her.

"I'm sorry for this, but I knew your husband," the man said extending his hand to Toritseju.

Toritseju was shocked. She didn't know him, and given that she was always on TV, it was possible for anyone to claim to know her husband, so she hesitated. But the next thing the man said changed her mind.

"We worked together with Chief Warebi," the man added. He must have noticed her hesitation.

"Oh my God," Toritseju found herself saying even as she felt her knees weaken. Other than the condolence messages and cheque of a million naira that the Chief had sent to her to 'help cover the burial expenses' as he had put it in the note that had come with it, Toritseju had never met the Chief.

"Please may I sit down? I'm so sorry for your loss," the man said as he took a seat beside Little Jolomi, putting the child between the two.

"Thank you. I'm sorry if I hesitated earlier. People know me, and I have received a lot of pity-stares in the last half hour just sitting here," she said managing a smile.

"I understand. I'm Tonye Kemefa. It's such an honour to meet you," the man said.

"Thank you Mr. Kemefa. You said you worked with my husband, were you also a journalist?"

"Oh no. I am a lawyer. I was a legal adviser to Chief Warebi. Anyway, that was ages ago, I resigned, as you must imagine, given the times, and I had to leave the city."

"Oh. I see. I left Warri too, soon after I heard of Jolomi's death."

"That was so sad. I didn't know about it until I saw your interview about a year or so after that. And I was in London at that time. I watched it on the BBC."

"Oh. It went all the way out there," Toritseju said and managed a blushing smile.

"Well, it did. Hello," the man said turning to look at Little Jolomi who for some reason had been silent all this while.

"I'm sorry; this is my son Jolomi Junior," Toritseju introduced the shy little man.

"Oh my. He's a striking resemblance of his father."

"I know. I had him after Jolomi left," Toritseju said. She didn't have any sign of sadness on her face.

"Wow. That's wonderful. Carrying on his legacy is the best way to immortalize him."

"Thank you so much Mr. Kemefa."

"You are welcome. You can call me Tonye please."

"Okay. Tonye."

"So where are you heading to?" he asked.

"London. The UN together with the BBC is giving Jolomi a posthumous award for excellence. That's what we are attending."

"Oh my! This is wonderful news. When is it? I must attend it. The best I can do."

"It's in a few days. So, you are also…"

"Yes, I am going to London too. Me and my assistant. Where is he anyway?" Tonye asked twisting his neck to look around.

"Oh. Maybe he's caught up with trying to check in."

"I doubt that."

"So, what do you do?" Toritseju found herself asking.

"I used to be Chief of Staff to Senator Matthews Ogheneovo. My assistant is taking over me for a while till he proves himself or is replaced by someone more competent." Tonye offered.

"Oh. That's good. I'm sure he will do fine."

"Well, my ex-boss doesn't think so. The senator insisted I babysit him and take him along on my vacation while I teach him the ropes. He's a bright lad. Ah, here he comes."

As soon as Toritseju saw him she recognized him. She would never forget that face. The kindness and warmth that it brought to her in those early hours when her grieving had started and that is aside the fact that he was the one who had broken the news of the death of her husband to her.

"Doctor Toju Benson?" The young man said in utter surprise as he saw her.

"Ah, I see my assistant is also a fan," Tonye said wondering why Oyinmiebi had so much familiarity on his face.

"It's not that Mr. Kemefa, this here is the same man who brought me Jolomi's bag and camera and all the stuff in it. He broke the news to me," Toritseju said as she stood up to take Oyinmiebi's extended hand.

"Oh. This is getting interesting," Tonye said.

"Indeed, it is and too good to be true," Toritseju said as she sat down again holding herself from bursting out in tears.

"Are you alright?" Tonye asked.

"I'm fine. You don't know how much this means to me. Today of all days when I'm going to London to witness Jolomi get the recognition he deserved. First, I meet you Tonye, and now this young man whose name I can't even remember."

"I didn't give it to you ma," Oyinmiebi said smiling from ear to ear.

"You didn't? Why?" Toritseju asked.

"Because I thought that the police would go looking for me thinking I killed your husband."

"I'm sorry but I don't understand what is going on. How did you come about Jolomi's bag?" Tonye asked turning to look at his assistant.

"It's a long story boss. One I am willing to share on the plane. But right now, I think this is our call," Oyinmiebi said springing to his feet as a voice from a PA system announced that their flight was ready to board.

Toritseju watched as Tonye lifted Little Jolomi who had fallen asleep soon after he saw that the discussion was too boring for him to take part in and carried him, resting the boy's head on his shoulder. She knew that there was a lot more to this man that she didn't know and somehow, she was keen on knowing more.

Months later after Toritseju relocated to London to take the new job and while she and Tonye had started seeing each other more, she would ask him to open his world to her and Tonye would tell her his story. And he would end his story by saying "I won." And years after that she would ask why he had said that, and he would say, "I ended up with the right Itsekiri woman for me and now I have two children of the same age." And they would laugh into the dead of the night while Tamaralayefa would be having sleepovers with her friends from school and Little Jolomi who wouldn't be so little anymore would be in his room playing computer games.

Eighteen.
May 2003.

THE STENCH TORE INTO Oyinmiebi's nostrils
without mercy as he followed the prison guard who was
leading him to see his client. As he walked on the slimy
grounds of the isle lined on both sides with cells
occupied by criminals, who once walked the society as
free men, he wondered the state in which his client
would be this time. The last time he had come to see
him, his client had been in a better cell and yet he wasn't
looking so good. His eyes were sunken; he had bruises all
over his body and every time Oyinmiebi had asked him
what had happened he had refused to say more.
Oyinmiebi wondered what he would look like now, given
that he had moved to join these prisoners.

With one hand holding his laptop bag as if his life
depended on it – his life did depend on it– Oyinmiebi
took his other hand to his nose and covered it as the
smell forced its way like savage vagabonds into his entire
system. The state of the prison hadn't changed for the
better over the years. He remembered his first tour of
this very prison years ago while he was still at the

university. The same old dump, the prison was.

He turned from side to side to look into the hungry eyes of the prisoners who looked like their spirits shattered beyond repair. He wondered how most of these people would function when or if they ever got out and would face the outside world they had gone through. A prisoner stuck his hand out through the iron bars of his cell and stretched it towards Oyinmiebi as the former hurried along. Oyinmiebi could overhear the prisoner say, *"tell my people I am alive"* and the young lawyer wondered what his story was and how long he had been in lock-up.

Oyinmiebi was relieved when the prison guard stopped in front of a huge metal door and began to sort out the large bunch of keys in his hand. They might have walked down the slimy isle for hours as far as Oyinmiebi was concerned.

He kept wondering why his client transferred to that run-down cell block.

The heavy metal door of the visiting area swung open amidst a heavy rusty clanging sound and the guard led Oyinmiebi right in. As he walked in, Oyinmiebi could see the back of his client hunched in total dejection. The large room was empty. It was not the regular visiting day. Oyinmiebi had pulled a lot of strings to be able to visit his client that day.

"Thank you, sir. I'm fine from here," Oyinmiebi said to the guard as he squeezed a hundred-naira bill into the grumpy old man's sweaty palm.

"Ok. I will be outside the door in case you want me,"

the guard said and left Oyinmiebi alone with his client. Oyinmiebi heard the heavy metal door close and lock behind him but he didn't mind. He knew he was safe. He knew his client more than anyone could ever understand or imagine. Or so he hoped.

As he walked towards the man, he wished the news he bore would make all the difference this time.

"Zuokumo," Oyinmiebi called as he got to a few feet from him. The prisoner heaved and turned.

"Oh my God Zuokumo, what is happening to you in here?" Oyinmiebi asked as he wondered if he should go and hug his cousin or keep his distance as the warden had warned earlier while he was making the visiting arrangements.

"Oyinmiebi, how are you? You are looking good today," Zuokumo said in broken English and his voice sounded even weaker and shakier than the last time.

"I am fine Zuokumo. I have some good news for you."

"Are you ready to represent me now?" Zuokumo asked. Oyinmiebi could hear a sneer in his voice.

"I cannot represent you Zuo. I told you how much of a conflict of interest this would be for me and my boss. But I was able to get a colleague of mine who would."

"Why do you hate me like this?" Zuokumo said instead.

"What are you talking about? Haven't I been doing everything I can to get you out? The other three times they arrested you, who got you bailed and got all the charges dropped? I did."

Zuokumo didn't say more.

"I work for the man whose property you and your brothers-at-arms destroyed, so I'm in a significant risk myself, by being here."

Zuokumo was silent.

"How are you being treated here?" Oyinmiebi asked.

Zuokumo remained silent.

"My colleague will see that you get a good trial."

Zuokumo remained unmoved. More hunched now than he was before.

"You will have to talk to me at some point Zuokumo. How else do you want me to help you if I cannot understand you or what drives you to keep doing these things after all that we have been through?" Oyinmiebi was tired. He didn't know what to do about his cousin.

Zuokumo had fallen into a deep depression after the violent outrage they had experienced in 1997. Oyinmiebi didn't know how involved Zuokumo had been in the Warri Crisis until one day he had overheard him talking in his sleep and when he had tried to wake him up, Zuokumo had jumped up and attacked him, almost strangling him, had his father not come to his rescue. Much later, when Zuokumo's manic depression started becoming more serious than they had imagined, he had called Oyinmiebi and had confessed to him all the things he had been involved in. And they were things Oyinmiebi never wished to remember.

Soon after, Zuokumo slipped into a serious mental illness, needing institutionalization. During that time, Oyinmiebi was studying at the Nigerian Law School in Abuja. After two years of being away from home Oyinmiebi returned to hear that Zuokumo had received the treatment he needed and had long left the institution but had gone on his way. Oyinmiebi's first encounter with his cousin after 1997 was in this same prison. And that was the beginning of their new relationship: Zuokumo would get himself into serious trouble and Oyinmiebi, who by that time had started working as a community organizer for Senator Matthew's campaign organization, would go out of his way to bail him.

Oyinmiebi was tired of it all. Their lives have taken two opposite turns and as much as it pained him; he was tired of carrying dead weight which would end up jeopardizing his own integrity.

Just then his phone began to vibrate in his breast pocket. He turned away from his cousin as he brought out his cell phone.

"Hello. Anna what's it?" He asked. It was his boss' secretary.

"The boss wants to see you. Where are you?" She asked.

"I'm just around the corner. I'll be back at the guesthouse in a few minutes," Oyinmiebi lied.

"You have to be here right now. They *both* want to see you."

"Both? You mean the *boss's* boss also wants to see me?" He asked. He wondered what the senator wanted with him. His direct boss was the Senator's Chief of Staff and he ever dealt with the Senator or the both at the same time for that matter.

"Yes Oyinmiebi, both. You do realize that you didn't come from Abuja to visit old friends, right. Get here now," she said. Anna was also a lawyer and she was his senior in the bar, which was the only reason Oyinmiebi tolerated the way she always talked to him.

"I am on my way Anna. And I am not visiting 'old friends,' I'm working."

"Whatever. Just get back here," she said and hung up.

Oyinmiebi wondered what her problem was. It was no secret that she'd wanted his job since she had graduated from Law School a year before him. But it was also no secret that the Senator himself had handpicked him when he had heard him give speech years ago, while organizing for another local politician.

After the woman hung up, Oyinmiebi turned and his heart jumped into his mouth. Zuokumo had been standing right behind him – for how long he had no idea. Their heads were just inches away and Oyinmiebi could see the blood in his cousin's eyes and he could also smell the stench coming from his body and breath. He jumped and found himself a few steps away as soon as he had turned.

"Jesus! Zuokumo you scared the hell out of me," Oyinmiebi said holding his chest as his heart wouldn't stop pounding.

"I always knew you were destined for wonderful

things," Zuokumo said.

Oyinmiebi tried to contain himself as fear began to grip him. That night came back to him. The night Zuokumo tried to strangle him.

"Zuokumo why don't you sit down let's talk. I don't have much time left," Oyinmiebi managed to say.

He saw that Zuokumo was trying to come closer to him, but he wasn't moving. It was then Oyinmiebi noticed that his cousin dangled from an iron hook shooting out of the concrete floor and the chain had just enough allowance to where he stood. Oyinmiebi wondered what could have happened if the chain hadn't been there. He didn't dare to think about it.

"Oyinmiebi, please go," Zuokumo said as he went back to his seat amidst the clings and clangs the chains made.

"What do you mean?" Oyinmiebi asked watching his cousin return to his former hunched position.

"I'm better off here. This is where I am meant to be."

"How could you even think that? You have no idea what your mother is going through. You need to get yourself some good rehabilitation and do something with your life," Oyinmiebi said and Zuokumo never spoke again until the grumpy old guard began to hit on the metal door to announce that their time was up.

"I'll send my colleague to help you. Get your life together," Oyinmiebi said and walked out. He didn't know if he was angry or just disappointed, or if now he just felt indifferent. He'd done what he could do and now it was time he went on with his life.

Oyinmiebi would never see Zuokumo again after that meeting in the visiting of the prison. On his arrival from London months later, he would learn that Zuokumo had gone into a rage and had run his head into the walls of his prison cell causing a serious brain aneurism. He had died three days later. Oyinmiebi spent years mourning the loss of his beloved cousin, blaming himself for giving up on him too easily.

"Oyinmiebi I don't understand why you would just leave without even telling me where you were going?" Tonye asked in anger as Oyinmiebi walked into the guest house where they were all staying while in town for the Senator's mother's funeral.

"I'm sorry sir. I went to get some antivirus into this," Oyinmiebi said tapping the laptop bag hanging around his shoulders.

"Oh. Ok. Please sit down. We have to see the Senator, but before we go in, I have some great news to tell," Tonye said.

Oyinmiebi could not read the expression on his boss' face as usual but he had a good feeling about it all. Like Voltaire once said, "in the case of news, we should always wait for the sacrament of confirmation."

Epilogue.

Bonfires of the gods!

I opened my eyes and all I saw was darkness. Thick and endless darkness that reached on into infinity. I could not make out if I was standing, or sitting, or lying down or just floating in the nothingness of oblivion that was *Duwamabou*.

At last, I had made it to *Duwamabou*, but it was nothing like what our forefathers had handed down to us in all the stories we heard while growing up. It was nothing like the beautiful land of the halfway house where the undead went to handle their unfinished business before moving on to the afterlife – wherever that was will remain a mystery to me. It was nothing like the place we dared to make up in our young imaginations while we sat by the fireplace and listened under the fullness of the new moon.

Duwamabou did not offer me the luxury of a single ray of light.

Was that death?

How long was I going to be there? I wondered, as I

remained static in that state - not moving or not knowing that I was moving.

I tried to call out my grandmother's name, but my voice did not respond to me. Grandmother was not here. I was alone. Lost in the deepest part of my own insanity. I was in deep slumber. I had to wake up now before I fell in any deeper.

I realized something. I crouched on all fours. I could feel my hand touching the ground, or whatever it was that I was on. I could also feel my knees. But other than the fact that I could *feel* that I had a pair of hands and knees, I still couldn't feel anything else. Then my eyes began to adjust to the darkness and far ahead of me, I could see a tiny speck. It was too dark for me to make out what it was, but I had no intention of just still being there, I had to go to it to find out what it was. Only one thought came to my mind now: I had to move forward, towards the mysterious speck.

I began to crawl. At first, I thought I was not moving forward since the darkness was so enveloping me, but I soon realized that the speck looked a little clearer than before.

I moved even faster now.

Now it was clear to me what the speck was; it was a hole in the veil of the oblivious darkness letting in a tiny ray of light. My heartbeat increased as I began to race towards it.

I don't know for how long I crawled, before I got to the speck, but it was soon right in front of me. I did not pant or catch my breath. My hands and knees did not hurt. It did not seem like I had been crawling for an eternity to get there. I was just there in what seemed like a split second, which had gone on forever.

I reached out to the speck and was glad when I touched a wall. I could feel the softness of the velvet darkness before me. I stuck a finger into the speck and it went right in. I began to wriggle my finger to widen the hole and soon my entire fingers were in. I began to yank and pull until the veil began to tear.

As soon the veil tore open, the eager and violent light raced against the darkness. I sat stuck in the middle. The battle between them was so fierce and blinding that I had to cover my eyes from getting blinded. After my eyes adjusted to the sudden rush of brightness, I looked around me. I was on my feet now.

Before me lay a vast waste land that seemed to go on into eternity.

I began to walk.

I began to go through the various stages of recovery from my present state of disillusionment. But I had no idea how I was going to come about it.

Just as I had appeared at the edge of the dark veil, I found myself at the end of the desert. It was a beautiful sight.

I could not hold my joy. I jumped up in the air in jubilation and soon after, I found myself running like a wild dog towards a beautiful lake that seemed to be flowing with milk and honey.

I must be in the Garden of Eden. I thought within myself as

I reached the edge of the lake.

I stooped over and began to scoop water with my palms into my mouth. The water tasted like nothing I had tasted ever before. It was delicious and alluring.

That was when I saw it.

At first, I saw its reflection right in the middle of the lake and it was magnificent.

I looked up to behold the most beautiful and majestic mountain I had ever seen anywhere in my entire existence. There must've been something about the mountain because as soon as I set my eyes on it, I found myself drawn towards it by invisible hands groping at me and pulling me.

I did not take my eyes off the mountain until I was standing at its foot. I looked up and the mountain went on up into the clouds.

A flight of stairs appeared leading up onto the mountains.

It was an invitation. I began to climb.

The steps were infinite, and I kept climbing putting one foot ahead of the other and this time I felt everything in the entirety of my being. I could feel my chest heaving up and down as I struggled to catch my breath. My legs were weakening but I could not stop climbing.

I climbed for a long time. I cannot remember now for how long I kept putting one foot in front of the other. I found the will, from somewhere divine, to go on and keep climbing.

As I approached the top of the mountain the climate changed. It became so cold. I hugged myself and increased my pace. Further to the top, I could hear sounds. Voices. Laughter.

At last! Perhaps *this* was *Duwamabou!* I thought to myself as I approached the top of the mountain. I began to feel the warmth that emanated from the mountaintop.

Fire. They had a fireplace. The cold was unbearable, so I could not wait to join them in their splurge around the fireplace.

I was excited. I would see my grandmother. I imagined.

At the top of the mountain which was a vast land, I saw them hurdled over a large bonfire made with large trunks of trees. The flames flickered and the woods and sticks that fuelled them creaked, as the bonfire sent thick smokes further up into the clouds. I took one step forward but stopped.

I had not noticed the barb-wired fence that surrounded the entirety of the mountaintop so when I tried to go through, the thorns pricked me.

I winced and that was when they noticed me.

They were three faceless beings huddled around the bonfire.

One turned to me and voice emanated from it.

"What do you want with us?" It asked.

"I don't know. I think I'm lost," I said

"Where do you want to be?" It asked.

"Duwamabou?" I wasn't so sure anymore.

It stopped talking and all three of them began to laugh.

"You don't want to be there my child," another voice came.

"Why?"

"Because you do not know the way there yet."

"Who are you?" I asked.

"Well, we are cold, and we need to keep warm," the third voice said.

"But who are you?" I asked again looking at them through the barb-wired fence that was the only thing that separated me from them.

"We are the gods of the Earth," the first voice said again. "Now be on your way," It said, and they vanished.

I was sweating when I opened my eyes. I was lying down strapped to a hard metal bed. I wriggled my body to try to break free until the loose ropes with which I stood tied gave way. I sat up and looked around me. There were many other people like me all sleeping and tied to their metal beds. What was this place? I wondered. I stepped off my metal bed and onto the cold floor and I felt pain in my chest. I winched but I was fine. Then I noticed something like a card attached to my big toe. I bent down and yanked it off. I read the message and my eyes widened.

It read, *"John Doe 27"*.

My heart began to race as it became clear to me. I was in a mortuary. They mistook me for a dead man. Or I had been dead and had just come back to life. I had no idea. I looked around for a door and began to make my way towards it as soon as I found it. I felt a little pain in my chest but other than that, I felt fine. I felt alive.

I was alive! Alive, not dead. And I was not a *John Doe*, I had a name. I was a living person.

I pushed the mortuary door open and stepped onto a corridor filled with wounded people lying everywhere. I walked past them and then past the empty nurses' station, out of the hospital and into the bright of day. The city was agog and more beautiful than I had imagined. People went about on all sides laughing and playing. Young and old lovers held on to each other by the side of the road. I inhaled fresh air and filled my lungs with it like I was saving it for the rainy days; I didn't want to let it out.

Just then I began to hear someone call my name. The voice was ever so familiar. I turned around to look for her. But I couldn't find her.

How could it be? But I already knew the answer even before I asked the question.

"Somina, what are you doing here?" Her voice was clear as crystal behind me. That sweet voice that sang me wonderful and sonorous lullabies when I was a little boy. That same voice that scolded me whenever I misbehaved or played in the rain with my friends. That same voice that would give me the best advice a grandson could ever ask for.

Oh! How I'd missed her voice.

I turned and there, standing in all her beauty, wearing the same beautiful white dress in which we buried her, was my grandmother. I rushed into her arms before I let reality set in.

"Mama, I'm so sorry," I said as I began to weep.

"It is okay my dear. Welcome my child. Welcome to Duwamabou," she said.

Made in the USA
Middletown, DE
10 January 2019